Axel

Book Three in the Ride Series

Megan O'Brien

Axel, The Ride Series
Copyright © 2015 Megan O'Brien

Print ISBN: 978-0-9996535-1-7

Megan
O'Brien
Books

To my family for being...everything.

To Mande, Mariah and Becky, thank you for reading my rough drafts, somewhat done drafts and the drafts that are in-between. You rock.

To my readers, you are all so amazing! Thank you for loving these characters as I love them, and in some instances, maybe more! I love being on this ride with you. XO.

Finally, to all those I've encountered along the way who have been so supportive of my love for writing romance – even those who don't read the genre! The support has been overwhelming, humbling and just plain cool.

Prologue

The sun's rays beat down on my skin in an unforgiving onslaught as I lay by the lake watching birds circle in the sky. It was close to summer in Nevada and though the heat was nothing like my native New York, it could still be oppressive. The heat was drier here though, not as humid and I was thankful for small mercies.

I could almost drift off, listening to the soft lapping of the water on the shore, the birds calling and the muted conversation all around me.

Freezing water dropping onto my bare belly broke me away from my reverie as I shrieked, sitting up in surprise.

"Just making sure you're awake, sis," Wes chuckled as his wife, Connie, socked him in the side.

"Happy now?" I asked with a raised brow, sitting up with a huff. Wes loved to tease me. Though I was Sal's little sister, he frequently treated me as an older brother would.

"Thrilled," he winked, throwing a muscled arm over Connie and kissing her temple.

I rose with a sigh, stretching my arms overhead and eyed the glistening lake and mountains beyond. Since Wes had so kindly introduced me to the temperature of the water, I might as well go in.

I ditched the jean shorts I'd been wearing over my bathing suit and headed to the water's edge. It felt cool but refreshing against the heat of the day and I wandered in to waist height before finally feeling brave enough to submerge entirely. I floated on my back for a short while, embracing the silence as my ears fell beneath the surface of the water. It made me want to tune everything out, to feel the abyss underneath. I took a deep, fortifying breath and dove under, relishing the burn in my lungs and the booming silence below.

There never seemed to be enough air for me on the surface anyway.

I forced myself to stay under, my lungs screaming in protest as my long hair fanned out around me.

Before I'd even fully embraced the quiet, I was aware of a disturbance in the water. Then firm hands gripped my arms, pulling me roughly to the surface.

I sputtered and took a few deep breaths before meeting the blazing grey eyes before me.

Axel.

No matter how much time I'd spent around him, he still made my heart sputter like an old motor before it revved to life, ready for flight.

"What the fuck are you doin'?" he demanded harshly.

"Uh, swimming?" I answered. Axel always put me in a state of confusion, no matter the occasion.

"Swimming typically involves your head above water," he fumed, his hands still gripping my arms.

"Yeah, well, I was trying something new," I retorted, still gasping a bit for breath.

The truth was, I didn't know what I'd been doing other than trying to escape my thoughts for a little while.

"Yeah, well, try something new out of the water then," he grumbled, pulling me with him to the pebbled shore.

I didn't answer him but followed dutifully, plopping on a towel and glaring briefly at my persistent savior.

He towered over me, his muscled frame glistening with moisture as his chest heaved from the exertion of his unnecessary rescue.

Connie sat down quietly beside me, her warm shoulder bumping mine in silent support. "What were you doing out there?" she asked quietly.

"Nothing." I shrugged, staring out at the water beyond.

"Didn't look like nothing," she murmured.

They all wanted me to talk. Desperately. Sal had demanded it time and time again. I knew they were all braced, as though I was a shoe waiting to drop.

My brother, technically half-brother, was part of a motorcycle club, something I'd known nothing about until I'd shown up on his doorstep. I'd since been thrust into their world, which I had to admit, most of the time was pretty sweet if not a bit overbearing. I'd grown fond of them all in a way I could have never anticipated. In getting to know my brother and loving him, I'd found that I loved the Knights and their women as well.

"I'm fine," I reiterated quietly.

"Okay, sweetie." She slung her arm around my shoulders, squeezing me briefly before letting me go.

Ettie, Mack's fiancée, came to sit next to me. They'd just become engaged a few days ago.

"Earth to Sophie," I heard her laugh a moment later.

"Hmm?" I asked distractedly as I sat transfixed,

watching Axel dry off. As the towel moved over every ridge of his six-pack and the broad plane of his chest, I'd never wanted to be a piece of fabric so badly in my life. The man was drool-worthy.

She nudged me with a small laugh. "See something you like?"

She had no idea just how much.

My cheeks flared as I forced my eyes away from him. "What were you saying?" I asked dreamily.

She rolled her eyes. "I was saying, I wonder if Sal and Kat are having a good time."

My brother and his fiancée, Kat, had gone to Spain a few weeks ago. They'd be back in just over a week.

"I'm sure," I nodded, my eyes turning back to Axel, watching as he threw a shirt on over his head. Clearly, he was getting ready to leave. I'd hoped to talk to him today, but it never seemed like a good time. Yet another day where things were clear as mud when it came to him.

Our relationship was so confusing, full of mixed signals and tension. It was also laced with a longing so intense, it was nearly tangible. I liked to believe that ran both ways.

He shot me a troubled look as though torn, before he reluctantly swung a leg over his bike and threw a two-fingered salute to Wes.

"He's an idiot," Connie put in.

"We both are," I muttered, watching as her brows knit at my comment.

Later that evening, I was just getting out of the shower when my buzzer rang. I was still staying in Kat's old apartment until I came up with another plan. "Hello?" I inquired, confused since I didn't expect anyone and was always on edge these days.

"It's me, Soph," Axel's gruff voice replied. "Let me up."

My heart stuttered in my chest as it always did when it came to him as I pushed the button, letting him up.

I pressed a nervous hand to my chest, cinching my robe tighter. When he knocked on my door, I forced myself to appear calm, outwardly at least, and opened the door to him.

He stepped inside; his large body making the space feel smaller and a good deal warmer as he dropped a pizza and a six-pack of beer on the counter.

"You brought dinner?" I asked with a raised brow.

He shrugged. "I thought you might be hungry."

I was in fact starving.

I peeked underneath the cardboard cover only to find he'd ordered my favorite. Hawaiian, yum.

"How'd you get home?" he asked, his muscular arms crossed over his broad chest.

His accusatory tone rankled me. He certainly hadn't offered to drive me home.

"What is this? The third degree? Can I at least put some clothes on?" I demanded.

He bit back a smile and nodded.

I huffed, moving toward my dresser, pulling out my sleep shorts and a tee, closing the bathroom door behind me to change.

I regarded myself in the mirror briefly. My cheeks held a crimson hue and my large brown eyes were alight with the familiar spark I'd never seen before this brawny man entered my life.

When I re-emerged, he'd made himself comfortable on the sofa, his motorcycle boots propped on the coffee table and beer in hand.

"Comfy?" I teased, grabbing a beer for myself.

His brows rose. "Do I look like a man who'd use the word 'comfy'?" he demanded.

I bit my lip trying not to laugh and shook my head, attempting to look remorseful for my use of such an apparently effeminate term. I practically snorted with my effort not to laugh.

"Jesus," he grumbled, trying to look put out, though his eyes twinkled with amusement.

"Why are you here?" I asked, dishing us up some pizza and coming to sit next to him on the sofa.

He shrugged. "Wanted to hang with you." He reached out for his plate, taking a big bite of the best pizza in town.

My cheeks warmed at his admission as I nodded, thrilled he wanted to spend time with me. The feeling was definitely mutual.

I cocked my head toward the TV Kat had so generously left behind. "Vikings again?" I asked, referring to the series we'd watched a few times together.

"Yeah," he agreed, his mouth full of food.

We'd been watching the show for nearly an hour; the sun had dipped low in the sky and I felt sleepy. Our plates had long since been discarded and my legs were pulled up underneath me as I lay on the opposite arm of the couch from where he was sprawled out.

As always, the energy in the room felt charged, at least for me. He was so close, this larger than life, beautiful man, just out of reach.

He seemed absorbed with the show, legs crossed at the ankle on the coffee table, hand resting on his abs. He never seemed as affected by being close to me as I was to him.

My heart pounded as I worked up the courage to talk

to him – to finally divulge the secret I'd held so closely. The secret that would change everything.

"Listen, Ax," I began, my heart hammering so hard it was nearly painful.

His eyes turned toward me expectantly.

"There's something I need to talk to you about." I licked my lips nervously.

The shrill ring of my phone began in the background but I ignored it, intent on the task at hand.

"Soph?" he prodded.

My phone rang again and I huffed in exasperation, rising to silence it.

I saw the familiar number flashing across the screen and was compelled to answer. I watched Axel wordlessly, memorizing the plane of his face, the color of his eyes, and the shape of his lips as I delivered the one-word answers that were required of me in a rushed whisper. It was only a five-minute conversation, despite it changing the course of my life.

I knew what I had to do.

I was on the next bus out of Hawthorne that very night.

Chapter One

Thirteen Months Later

"That order you've been waitin' on is up," Stacy, a fellow waitress, mentioned in passing as she snapped her gum.

"Thanks," I murmured, relieved. Table 12 had been giving me trouble since they sat down and it hadn't helped that their food had taken longer than usual.

Giovanni's was a popular little Italian place downtown with good food and a quiet atmosphere. I was lucky they'd given me the chance to waitress since I'd had no experience when I started.

"Do y'all need anything else?" I asked after I'd put the steaming plates down in front of four impatient gentlemen. The "y'all" had emerged somewhere in the last few months and I was rolling with it.

"Your phone number for starters," one of them returned without pause.

I fought the urge to roll my eyes.

A sing-song voice called out, "She's taken, honey." Dwayne swept in to rescue me as he gave me a wink and sashayed on down to pick up his own order.

"It's true," I nodded along with the lie Dwayne had become accustomed to dropping whenever one of the customers got overzealous.

"Too bad," the man replied, his eyes sweeping over my frame that in no way moved me or made my heart pitter or patter.

I feared that patter had been permanently lost to a certain bearded biker I'd left back in Hawthorne over a year ago.

"Anything else?" I pressed, looking deliberately at their glasses and plates full of food.

"We're good," one of the other men nodded, allowing me to sweep off to my next table.

By the time my shift ended, I was exhausted as always. I gathered my things and headed out, waving to Dwayne and the cooks as I left.

The humid air of the Texan evening hit me like a wet blanket. After nearly a year in the south, I still wasn't used to the humidity. It was even worse than my native New York, if that was possible.

Living in Texas was still so foreign to me. Everything was so big and overdone. But the people were kind and so friendly; it took months for me to realize it was genuine.

I stopped at my favorite taco stand to grab a quick bite. After nearly a year of working at an Italian restaurant, a girl could only eat so much pasta. I scarfed down my taco as I waited for my bus. I'd still never learned how to drive.

By the time I walked up to my apartment complex, I was dead on my feet. I worked damn hard to make ends meet.

I looked up at the complex I called home, and despite the slightly run down exterior, a familiar sense of pride warmed me, along with the oppressive heat. The place might not be the Upper East Side brownstone I'd grown up in, but it was mine.

I made my way up the exterior steps and down the short hall, skipping my apartment and knocking lightly on the one next door.

Familiar noises came from inside, making me smile.

Jill, my neighbor and only real friend, swung the door open looking slightly harried, but it was late; that was to be expected.

"Hi," I smiled, stepping into her place, my eyes sweeping the room in search of Maddox. He was sitting up on a blanket with his best buddy, Mason, both chewing heartedly on teething rings, drool dribbling down their chubby cheeks.

My son. My life.

"Hi, buddy," I grinned, kneeling in front of him. He was such a beautiful boy, every day I was struck by it. His complexion favored mine, slightly fair, but his hair was darker than my chestnut brown and was just starting to curl up as it came in. But it was his eyes that really set him apart. I never grew tired of looking into them. I had never known I could love the way I loved him.

"He did great today," Jill shared as she moved around the room picking up toys. "Want to stay for a late dinner?" she offered.

I shook my head, scooping my boy up. "I ate on the way and I'm exhausted. This weekend?"

"Sure," she agreed.

"Thanks, as always, you're a godsend," I said sincerely. Jill's husband traveled almost constantly for work and she frequently babysat Mad and a few other kids for extra income. She'd been a nurse before having Mason, but with Tim traveling so much, she stayed home full time. She was affordable, and more importantly, I trusted her.

When Maddox was born, I'd barely known how to take care of myself, let alone a baby. But Mad and I were making it work. It certainly wasn't how I'd planned for my life to go, but I didn't regret it, not for a second.

After saying goodbye, I let us in to our one-bedroom apartment, setting his diaper bag down on the small kitchen table.

I put him down with his toys on the blanket in the small living room and moved to the kitchen to get his milk ready before bed.

I chatted to him about my day, our one-sided dialogue, easily filling the quiet room with my voice and his babbling and giggles. I talked to my son more than anyone else. It was a minor miracle I could still successfully hold a two-way, adult conversation.

He looked up at me grinning when I brought his milk over, and as happened more than once a day, I felt a pang in my chest at how much he reminded me of Sal when he smiled.

I missed my brother.

I missed Axel most of all.

In all these months trying to forget, it was his face and his voice I heard every night before bed.

My heart was a glutton for punishment.

Those grey eyes were burned into my memory with a tenacity time and distance could not erase. Despite every effort to forget, I'd never felt for any man the way I'd felt for him. It was terrifying and consuming.

Maddox gurgled, reminding me I was spacing out

again, holding his milk. "Sorry, sweetie," I murmured, scooping his chubby body up in my arms and moving to the couch to feed him.

I watched him drink, my hand stroking over his soft hair as his eyes began to droop. My own eyes wanted to follow, but I forced them open long enough to finish up and put my sweet boy to bed.

He'd just started sleeping through the night. How I'd gotten through those first few months of him waking every few hours or better yet, nights he didn't sleep at all, I still didn't know.

I showered and dressed for bed, climbing in under my covers. Maddox slept in a small alcove in the living room that was meant to be an office space. I'd tried having him sleep in my room, but that didn't seem to work for either one of us. It wasn't like I had a social life that our living situation disrupted.

I was lonely, desperately so, and at times, terrified of the future. But I was also a hell of a lot stronger than I'd ever realized. I was proud of the woman I was, of the mother I'd been from the moment the nurses placed Maddox in my arms asking where his daddy was.

Chapter Two

"How about that guy from 3B?" Jill prodded as we sat on her couch, each with a glass of wine in hand. She was referring to our neighbor who'd asked me out repeatedly.

Both boys were crashed out in Mason's room. This was the only way either of us got a 'night out' and we took advantage whenever possible.

I wrinkled my brow and shook my head. "No spark," I sighed.

"You always say that." She rolled her eyes heavenward. Jill was beautiful and exotic looking with her Native American ancestry. Her dark hair shone with a gorgeous gloss I often had to reach out and touch. She was seven years older than me, but I'd never even noticed the age difference.

"Well, it's true," I defended with a huff.

"Soph," she sighed. "I know you don't like to talk about your past and you know I won't pry. But whatever it was – whatever it is, don't you think it's time to move on? You're gorgeous. You look amazing and you just had a baby six months ago– you lucky bitch," she snarked with a grin. "Go out, meet a hot man and let him take you to bed!" she coaxed.

I blushed and shook my head. My only experience with sex had started out amazing and ended with him freaking out with a capital F.

I thought back to that evening so often the binding of the book in my memory was well worn.

She rolled her eyes at me. "Fine," she sighed, as she always did when the subject came up.

"Tim's coming home soon," I put in, trying to distract her by mentioning her husband. He'd been gone for three months and was due back the following week.

"Yeah," she smiled, though it didn't touch her eyes. She didn't talk about Tim much and I'd never pried. God knows, I had my own secrets.

"I'm glad." I squeezed her hand briefly. "I'm beat, time for bed," I announced, rising to stretch. "I'll go sneak in and grab Mad," I said around a yawn.

"Thanks for hanging out," she smiled.

"Anytime." I grinned back with a wink. Jill was a true friend. It killed me that she could only know a piece of me, but I'd take what I could get.

I fell asleep that night thinking about that damned spark. I thought about how it was so fierce with Axel; it was almost a life force all its own. Maybe I'd just be alone forever since I couldn't seem to settle for anything less.

*****

"Bella, your order's up!" Dwayne called the next evening.

I rolled my eyes at the most southern man I'd ever known calling me 'Bella' but he'd done it from day one. We'd seriously discussed a name change for him over a bottle of Chianti one night, but had quickly moved on to discuss men, his favorite subject. The man was many things – someone who fit the name 'Dwayne' wasn't one of them.

To me, Dwayne was a name for a cattle rancher or maybe a mechanic down on his luck. It certainly didn't fit with my leopard print and sequin shirt-wearing friend whose hips swayed so dramatically when he walked, I was worried he'd end up with permanent damage.

The tips were great on weekends, and if I had to deal with prima donna Dwayne, then so be it. Truth be told, I sort of loved the guy. Though I'd never tell him that; he'd force that high-school musical movie marathon party on me, which he'd threatened me with from the moment we met. He promised it would be the best night of our lives. Unsurprisingly, I wasn't convinced.

"Got it," I answered, sweeping in to gather the steaming platters of eggplant parmesan and penne primavera.

When I turned to deliver the food, I nearly dropped it on the floor. Henry, the president of The Sinners, a motorcycle club who partnered often with the Knights, and his lady were sitting in front of a bottle of wine waiting for their food. I'd switched mid-shift with Betty and had no idea they were here until now.

"Shit," I breathed. I didn't think they'd seen me, but I spun on my heel nonetheless. "D, can you please deliver these to table 5," I hissed with panic.

"Why, sugar?" he asked, looking over my shoulder in question.

"Please, they're nice people. I just…I can't see them. Please?" I asked again, unable to curb my clear desperation.

He looked at me with concern before nodding. "Sure thing, sugar plum," he agreed, taking the platter from me and strutting his way to their table.

I hid out in the kitchen until Dwayne gave me the all-clear. He covered all my tables for that hour. I owed him a favor, which meant I'd likely be seeing a lot of Zac Efron in my future.

"Thanks," I sighed, shoving off from the counter I sat on.

"No problem, honey." He patted my leg and didn't ask anything more.

Another week went by. Mad was cutting a tooth so I was exhausted when I walked in that evening to start my shift. I felt like a zombie with a notepad as I moved from table to table.

"Table 10's a hottie!" Dwayne squealed with a wink. I gave him a small nod and with half a grin, headed in that direction.

"Can I take your order?" I asked, my eyes on my notepad.

"I'll have the lasagna – and you," the familiar voice answered.

My heart stopped. I gasped, my eyes wide, all exhaustion forgotten and replaced with adrenalin.

I looked up into familiar grey eyes and felt panic and lust all at once.

"Hi, Soph," he greeted, his tone calm, though his eyes glittered with an unspoken emotion.

He looked amazing. His hair was shorter, the familiar curls gone but his beard remained. He looked bigger, more muscular but it was possible I'd forgotten how big he'd always been.

"H-hi," I stammered. "What are you doing here?"

"What am I doing here?" he growled incredulously. "What the hell are you doing here, Sophie?" he demanded.

My eyes darted nervously around the restaurant. "You should go." My voice betrayed my worry.

"I'm not going anywhere," he shook his head, his eyes sweeping my frame.

"Ax, seriously. I left for a reason. A good one. You should go," I hissed.

"Can't," he shook his head.

My eyes narrowed. "What do you mean you can't?"

He leaned forward in the booth, his hand reaching out to clasp my wrist. "I've spent over a year tormented over you, Sophie. We are going to talk. And I'm not leaving until we do."

Oh, hell no. Just…no.

"Tormented over me?" I asked incredulously. "Since when? What?" I stammered, truly dumbfounded.

"That could be part of the talking portion." he shrugged.

He said it so casually as though his hot and cold behavior had been no big deal. It pissed me right the hell off.

"You never could decide what you wanted from me. I'm not the same girl you knew." I shook my head. "I don't have time for this. I advise you to go straight back to Hawthorne," I told him sternly, turning on my heel and rushing to the kitchen.

What was he even doing here? It had to have been Henry. I could have sworn he hadn't seen me. My heart was pounding so hard; I was worried I'd need an ambulance at this rate. I collapsed on the ground next to the stove, panting for breath. Another shift hiding out in the kitchen, great way to keep a job.

When the door swung open, I winced as his motorcycle

boots came into view. He heaved a sigh and crouched in front of me. "I knew this wouldn't be easy." His voice was gentle as he lifted my chin to force me to look in his eyes. "But, Soph, it's not just me. Your brother, Kat, all of us miss you like hell. We've been searching for you, worried about you for over a year. You're family. We're going to talk," he commanded, his beautiful eyes glittering with intensity.

I shook my head. "You should go."

"Everything okay in here, sugar?" Dwayne's high voice broke in.

I looked up at him in alarm. "Yes, fine. He was just leaving. Sorry, I'll get back to work."

Dwayne looked me over and met my eyes, cocking his head in question.

I nodded, letting him know I was really okay.

My eyes shifted back to Axel. "I have to get back," I murmured.

"I'll wait, drive you home after your shift," he stated, rising and pulling me to my feet. His touch alone sent electricity zinging down my arm.

"No!" I practically shouted in alarm at the thought of him driving me home.

His eyes narrowed. "You have a man at home?"

Yes, a very small one, I thought frantically.

He eyed me keenly, our intensity blistering as it always did. Some things never did change. "Do you?" he demanded quietly.

"No," I whispered.

"Good," he whispered back, his voice hoarse as he took me in.

"But you're not driving me home. It was good to see

you, Ax. Tell everyone…" my voice caught, "tell them I miss them and hope they're well." I gave him the small smile I'd like to think I'd perfected. The one I could plaster on my face despite inner desolation threatening to swallow me whole. I'd had to wear it most of my life. I pushed my way out of the kitchen to see about my tables.

I spent my entire shift alternating between plotting where Mad and I should move next and freaking out over how amazing it had been to see Axel. I felt like someone had taken my heart and injected it with steroids.

When I got off at eleven that night, I snuck out the back. It opened into a dimly lit alley and I thought I'd be golden if he was still waiting all these hours later out front.

"You think I'd wait out front?" he chuckled, his tone nearly affronted.

I jumped about a mile in the air and smacked him in the chest. "You scared me!" I screeched.

"Soph, seriously, give me more credit." He grinned through the dim light. "Let's go get a drink." He cocked his head toward the street.

I looked at him, biting my lip, debating whether I could realistically escape him. He stared back at me, watching my inner turmoil and allowing me to come to the only conclusion possible.

I sighed in defeat. "Fine. I just need to check on something," I responded, firing off a text to Jill.

She was annoyingly thrilled that I wanted to stay out later. She said the boys were already crashed out and I should take as long as I wanted. I responded, telling her that her amount of exclamations marks needed to be toned down.

Seriously.

"Fine, one drink," I agreed, going against my better judgment. "But," I held up a finger, "you're not driving me home."

"Whatever you want," he agreed – all too easily.

We walked in silence to a nearby bar I'd never been to. Sitting at the bar, side by side, he ordered us both a beer and swiveled slightly to face me.

"I'm so fucking glad you're okay. Christ, Sophie," he breathed, running a hand over his beard; something he always seemed to do when he was stressed.

"Yeah, I'm okay," I replied quietly.

"Why the hell did you take off like that? How could you do that to us?" he demanded heatedly.

I narrowed my eyes at him, the heat rising in my cheeks. "Us?" I demanded. "First of all, I feel like shit for leaving everyone – they were all so good to me," I swallowed. "I love my brother. It meant the world to me to get to know him in a way I never had before. Given all that, don't you think it's fair to assume I had my reasons?" I shot back.

"What the fuck about me, huh?" he growled.

"What about you?" I shot back passionately as his eyes narrowed. I took a deep breath, trying to bring down the intensity a bit. "Look, I don't want to fight. It is good to see you," I nodded. "I just...I feel stupid really, naïve," I shrugged.

"Why?" he asked when I'd paused, my embarrassment reaching a crescendo.

"I had thought maybe...maybe you and me..." I trailed off. "Sometimes the way you would look at me, I saw something there, but then you'd tell me I was too young or that I was Sal's sister. It was always mixed messages with you," I shook my head.

"We'll get to that," he interrupted. "I want to know why you left. What the hell are you doing in Texas?"

"We'll get to that," I retorted, throwing his words back at him.

We stared at each other in silent challenge before he nodded once and turned his gaze to his drink. I practically slumped back into my chair, relieved not to be the focus of his intensity for a few moments.

He completely undid me, always had.

"How are Sal and Kat?" I asked, unable to temper my curiosity and wanting to change the subject.

"They're good," he nodded. "They got married when they were in Spain," he told me, rocking my world.

"What! That's great!" I exclaimed, happy for my brother, while aching with regret that I'd missed so much.

"Yeah," he agreed.

"How's everyone else?"

"You should come home and see," he challenged.

"How are you?" I asked quietly, ignoring his comment.

He turned to me, his hand reaching out to sweep my hair back from my neck. That slight touch made me shiver. He didn't miss it. "I'll be a lot better when my girl's home where she belongs," he answered without preamble.

Uh, what?

"Since when…?" I trailed off, utterly shocked.

"Since always, Soph," he answered. "You and me, we have some shit to sort out. You need to tell me why you left and I need to prove to you that you're mine."

Oh, God, how I'd fantasized about hearing something like this from him. Now? Now I couldn't do anything about it.

"Ax, this isn't just about you and me," I swallowed over

the huge lump in my throat. "If it's guilt you're feeling or something like it, seriously, you can let that go. It's not why I left," I told him seriously. "I want you to be happy. I hope you will be."

He looked at me, his eyes searching through to my very soul. "You're telling me there's no chance for us – none?" he demanded.

I met his gaze, knowing I needed to. "None," I whispered.

"I don't believe you," he growled, vindication in his tone. No doubt he'd caught the lie in my eyes. He always seemed to be able to do that.

I looked at the time on my phone and winced. I knew Jill had it covered but Mad wasn't sleeping so well with his teething. "I have to go," I told him. "I'm sorry. It was good to see you," I said quietly, sliding off my barstool and delivering a quick kiss to his cheek.

I slipped out of there before he could stop me.

"Sophie!" I heard his deep voice holler when I'd reached the sidewalk.

I took a deep breath, bracing myself before turning to meet his gorgeous face.

"What?" I asked impatiently.

"This," his deep voice growled, pulling me into his big body with such force I had to put my hands up against his chest to stop from slamming into him.

Then his mouth was on mine with a kiss so consuming my knees literally went weak. His tongue stroked mine with beautiful skill, breaking only for his teeth to nip my lower lip, licking the sting away. His hands buried themselves in my hair tugging slightly as moisture pooled between my legs.

I wanted to climb up his body and claim him. I wanted him to lay me down and do the same.

We stood ravishing each other until I felt short of breath, until my lips felt raw and swollen.

Oh, but what delicious pain.

"You tell me now that there won't be an us," he challenged, his forehead pressed to mine.

I wanted to ask why he seemed so clear about things when he clearly hadn't been a year ago. I had so many questions. Mainly when he'd kiss me again.

But this wasn't about me.

"I have to go." My voice was hoarse and unrecognizable to my own ears.

I pulled away, taking a deep breath, trying to pull myself together – and failing miserably.

"This isn't over," he replied. "You and me, we're just starting."

I gave him a small smile. "I wish that were true." I replied, turning and walking away.

I caught a cab home in my rush, knowing I wasted nearly my entire evening's tips with the fare. I tapped quietly on Jill's door and went in to gather my boy and carry him home.

"Have fun?" Jill questioned with an excited whisper.

"You could say that, sort of," I answered vaguely. "Night."

I slipped out of her place with Mad sleeping on my shoulder, a blanket wrapped around his warm body.

As I moved to unlock my door, I saw movement in my peripheral vision. I gasped, dropping my keys on the ground, the clatter ricocheting off the concrete walls. Axel's formidable frame stole some of the light as he stood towering in the hallway.

He moved closer, his expression thunderous and confused. I held my fingers to my lips praying he wouldn't wake Mad. He nodded, his movement jerky as he eyed the sleeping bundle I carried.

I put the key in the lock and pushed inside. Axel seemed so big in our small space.

I went to put the baby to bed when he stirred. I braced, biting my lip hard. He lifted his body away from my chest and blinked, looking around the room.

When his eyes met Axel's, I knew it was all over.

Two pairs of identical grey eyes stared back at the other.

"Christ," Axel swore with emotion.

Maddox grinned his gummy smile and shoved a chubby hand into his mouth.

"Yeah," I murmured. "He's yours."

Chapter Three

"How? What?"

For the first time ever, the imposing Axel Black was speechless.

As it turned out, you could get pregnant your first time. We'd even used protection. I bit my lip, revealing what I'd known from the beginning. "The condom must have broken."

"But…" he stammered as Maddox grinned and cooed in my arms.

"It's okay, Ax, why don't you sit down on my bed?" I encouraged. He looked like he was about to faint. "Mad sleeps out here and I need to put him down," I explained.

"Mad?"

I met his confused gaze. "Maddox," I clarified quietly.

"My grandfather's name?" he whispered hoarsely.

His grandparents were the only family he'd ever spoken fondly of. It was the one thing I'd felt I could give him.

"Yeah," I nodded.

"Christ," he repeated, running a hand over his face.

"My bed, Ax," I repeated, with a tilt of my chin in that direction.

"Right," he muttered.

I put Maddox down, watching as his eyelids fluttered closed.

I straightened my shoulders, bracing myself for the hurricane waiting for me in my bedroom.

"How the hell could you not tell me?" he demanded in a strangled voice. He sat on the edge of my bed, his head in his hands.

"I wanted to," I said quietly. "I couldn't."

"Why the fuck not? That's my son! I missed how many months of his life?" he demanded.

"Six," I whispered.

"Six," he repeated. "I missed your being pregnant. Your labor. Fuck, tell me you weren't alone."

"I wasn't alone," I answered immediately.

He shot me a look.

"The nurses were really kind," I added with a sigh.

"What the fuck, Sophie!" he exploded.

"It's complicated," I tried weakly.

He narrowed his eyes at me.

"I know you'll probably never forgive me but I did what I thought I had to. To protect you. To protect Maddox," I explained passionately.

He stood suddenly, his size overwhelming as he stalked toward me. "You think there's anything I would let happen to you or our child? Do you think I'd let anything hurt you?" His voice was raw with pain.

"I think there are forces bigger than you and me." I swallowed, looking up at him. "And I think with that precious baby out there, I couldn't risk it," I whispered. "I did what I had to do to protect him. To protect you and my brother." My eyes filled with tears as I tried to explain what had made me run. "But that's all to hell now," I added, my voice raw.

He stumbled back to the bed, sitting as though drunk. "All that time in Hawthorne you were...you were..."

"Pregnant," I nodded. "I kept trying to tell you. But after the night we were together, you were so dodgy, so unsure."

"So this was revenge?"

I reeled back in shock. "No! God no. I kept trying to tell you. I thought I had time to work up to it. And then... and then the threats just became too much and I knew if I stayed, I'd just screw up your whole life and Sal's," I shook my head. "I couldn't allow that."

"So you what? Disappeared on your own to go through your entire pregnancy alone? To be a single mother when you could have had me? Could have had all of us?"

His comment pissed me right the hell off.

"Would I have had you? You tell me, after that night we spent together and how you treated me afterwards, how the hell do you think I should have thought that!" I exclaimed.

"You think so little of me?" He rose from the bed, his stance tense and expression thunderous. "You think I wouldn't take care of you and my child?"

"Lower your voice," I hissed.

"This is so fucked up," he groaned, raking his hand through his hair.

"Pretty much," I agreed. "But whatever was between us – whatever the hell that even was..." I sighed and he narrowed his eyes. "That has nothing to do with why I left."

"Yeah, we're gonna get to that," he declared.

I sighed, utterly spent and overwhelmed. "I know you

probably hate me," I murmured. "But Ax, I'm so tired. I don't even know what to say to you right now."

His grey eyes swept over my face and I was sure he was taking in the dark circles under my eyes and pale complexion.

He nodded, his expression cool. "We'll talk again in the morning."

"Where are you staying?" I asked with a yawn.

"Here," he answered with zero hesitation.

"I'm sorry, what?" I asked, dumbfounded.

"You and my son are under this roof and I'm not going anywhere." He shook his head with determination.

"There's nowhere for you to sleep!" I protested.

He eyed the bed with a cocked brow.

"There's nowhere for you to sleep," I reiterated with hands on my hips.

He sighed. "There's a perfectly good couch."

"Mad sleeps out there," I shook my head.

"I don't know much about babies, but Gracie always sleeps like the dead." He shared, speaking of Cole and Scarlet's little girl.

"He usually does," I allowed. "But he's cutting a tooth."

"It's fine," he shrugged. "I've got lots of time to make up for."

My eyes filled with tears as I whispered hoarsely, "I didn't do this to hurt you. I swear it."

He gripped the back of my neck, his eyes blazing down into mine. "Yeah, I'm counting on that."

Then he was gone and I was left standing in my bedroom, listening to him quietly move around the living room.

Despite my exhaustion, I tossed and turned, worried

about what his return could mean. I knew Axel well enough that once he saw our son, he'd never let go. I just had to hope we'd both survive what was to come.

I woke up late the next morning, jolting out of bed at seeing that the clock read 8 a.m. I hurtled out of my room worried for Maddox.

I was met with two identical sets of grey eyes looking up at me when I stopped abruptly in the living room, the past evening flooding back to me.

Axel sat with Mad in his lap at the kitchen table.

"I didn't know what he ate," he shrugged. "But he seems to like my banana," he added with a grin as Maddox opened up to gum another bite.

I felt my entire being soften at watching the two of them together. "Yeah, he likes bananas," I responded, feeling a tenderness toward him that up to this point, I'd only felt for Maddox. "He just started on some solid food."

"I made coffee." Axel cocked his head toward the coffee pot.

"Thanks," I murmured gratefully, dropping a brief kiss on Mad's head before moving to fill up a cup. "Can I get you a refill?"

"No, I'm good." He shook his head, his eyes watching me move around the small space as I made Maddox his bottle.

"Do you want to feed him?" I asked quietly, handing him the warm bottle.

"Yeah," Axel nodded, his expression unreadable as he took the bottle and gave it to Mad.

A knock sounded at the door and I saw Axel stiffen. "It's just Jill," I assured him, moving to open the door. Jill stood on the other side with Mason balanced on her hip.

She breezed into the room.

"Is there coffee because this little stinker was up all…" She stopped mid-sentence, her mouth hanging open when she spotted Axel.

"Jill, this is Axel. Maddox's father," I introduced a bit awkwardly. The words weighed heavily in the air. I looked over, seeing a storm of emotion pass over Axel's face at being referred to as a dad.

"Hi," she choked out, her eyes wide with shock.

"Hey." He gave her a chin lift, continuing to hold the bottle for Maddox who was sucking greedily.

"Are you still bringing Mad over while you go to work?" she asked me with wide eyes.

"Yes," I answered at the same time Axel answered, "No."

I glared at him.

"You okay, Soph?" she asked quietly; I could tell she was worried. I'd never spoken a word about Axel to her or the fact that he was a formidable biker with tattoos and a gruff personality.

"I know there's a lot I haven't told you," I responded regretfully. "But I trust him. I'm good." I assured her.

She peered around me with a shrewd gaze. "You gonna take care of my girl here because for a twenty-five year old, she lives like an old spinster," she huffed and I rolled my eyes.

"I'm gonna take care of both of them," he replied, meeting her skeptical gaze.

She gave an affirmative nod. "Okay, maybe I like him." She headed to the coffee pot after putting Mason down on the baby blanket. Mad immediately started to squirm.

"He wants to sit with his best bud," I told Ax, taking

him from his lap and setting him down next to Mason.

"So how long are you in town for?" Jill asked Axel lightly.

"As long as it takes to get her to come home with me," he answered without hesitation.

My eyes bugged out of my head at his declaration.

"Where's home?" Jill asked with confusion.

I winced, again feeling guilt over how little I'd told her.

"Nevada," Axel answered for me.

I'd only spent a short time there, but it was true. Nevada felt more like home to me than New York. Texas certainly had never quite fit. But all that didn't mean returning was a smart move.

Jill cleared her throat. "Okay then, clearly you two have some things to work out." She shot me a wry look. "I'll just head back over to my place and we'll talk later?" she questioned me with a raised brow.

"Yeah," I murmured. "Let Axel and me talk. Mad might be over later," I told her.

She nodded as Axel's eyes narrowed. "Nice to meet you. My husband gets back this weekend. Don't make him come kick your ass," she warned Axel.

He chuckled, his demeanor lightening for the first time. "I'll try."

"She's a good friend," I told Axel after she'd scooped Mason up and shut the door behind her.

"Seems it," he muttered, his eyes on Maddox.

"What's going on here, Axel?" I blurted before I could stop myself.

"Seems like you're going to go to work and I'm gonna watch our boy," he stated matter-of-factly.

My eyes filled with unexpected tears. "But I've never

left him with anyone but Jill. And you're mad at me and…"
I trailed off.

He stood, crowding my space, his face peering down into mine. "Mad doesn't even cover it," he countered. "I wish like hell you would have trusted me to take care of you. To protect you. I wish you hadn't made this decision on your own that took you and my boy from me. I've lost a lot of time. But as mad as I am, remember that I came here for you, Soph, before I even knew about Maddox." His voice dropped an octave as he continued. "The reasons I came back haven't changed."

I looked up into his earnest eyes and reluctantly nodded, biting my lip to the point of pain.

"He, um, he'll need a nap at noon after he eats lunch," I trailed off, looking to the side before giving him further instruction. This whole thing was so surreal. I felt so vulnerable leaving Maddox with anyone, even his daddy.

"Got it," Axel nodded after I'd rattled off every instruction I could think of.

"Please call me if you have any questions," I stressed. "And, Jill always knocks exactly how she did this morning. Anything else – don't answer the door," I said firmly, feeling mildly panicked at the thought.

He tipped my chin up. "Baby, it's okay. I'm here. No one's gonna get to you or Maddox," he assured me.

"Okay," I whispered.

"See you when you get home," he murmured, watching my movements as I flew around the room gathering my things for my lunch shift at the restaurant.

"This is hard," I whispered, tears filling my eyes again as I leaned down to kiss Maddox. I stood to face Axel. "I know I need to trust you. I know I robbed you of so much.

But he's all I have in the world," I rasped, wiping my face and trying to pull myself together.

"Soph, I would never ever take him from you, if that's what you're worried about," he said quietly, zeroing in on my true fear. "And he's not all you have. You have me, too. You always did."

Holy....wow. I wasn't even sure what to do with that statement.

"Okay," I agreed, knowing with crushing clarity that from that moment on, my life would never be the same.

Chapter Four

If a day could move any slower, they'd call it a month. Despite a busy lunch rush and texting Axel off and on all day, the day had dragged.

I rushed home just as the blistering sun was dipping in the sky, ready to hold my baby.

I heard commotion coming from my apartment as I neared the stairwell which made my feet move faster, running up the stairs and bursting through my front door in alarm.

What I found on the other side shocked me to the core.

It looked as though all the senior members of the Knights' Motorcycle Club sat in my tiny living room with their women, though my brother and Kat were noticeably absent. Scarlet and Cole, Wes and Connie, Ettie and Mack all sat in various spots around the room.

"Oh, my God," I breathed, my eyes shooting through the room until I spotted Mad sitting on his blanket with who must be Gracie toddling nearby.

She was walking? I couldn't believe how much I'd missed.

"She's walking," I said dumbly, the door still hanging open behind me.

"Yeah," Scarlet replied with a warm smile, standing to embrace me.

I couldn't help it; she'd always been like a big sister to me. So comforting and accepting. I started to bawl like a baby.

"I missed you guys so much. But you shouldn't be here!" I exclaimed through tears, worried beyond measure.

"Oh, honey, where else would we be? He's so beautiful!" she gushed. "He and Gracie are best friends already," she laughed, patting me soothingly.

"Where's my brother?" I asked hoarsely.

"Here," his deep voice surprised me from behind.

Scarlet released me, stepping back as I whirled to face Sal and Kat. They'd just arrived, bags on their shoulders.

Sal and I stared at each other for a moment before he stepped forward and pulled me into a bone-crushing hug. "Don't you ever pull this shit again, Sophie, I swear to God," he swore at me.

"Sorry," I rasped as I was pulled out of Sal's embrace and into Kat's.

"What he said," she warned, her bark holding less bite.

I drew back against the bump I felt. "Oh, my God! Are you…?"

She nodded with a grin. "About six months along now."

"Congrats," I whispered.

"Thanks," she winked, pulling back to take a good look at me.

Mad whined then, pulling my attention away as everyone looked over at him. I crossed the room, scooping him up. He wasn't used to so many people and his eyes were larger than normal as he looked around the room.

The room grew unnervingly quiet as my brother stared at my little boy. His dark eyes swept to me then to Axel, then back again.

"What. The. Fuck," he seethed, glaring at Axel with such hostility I worried they'd come to blows at any second.

Axel's countenance remained calm as he met my brother's anger head on. Then his grey eyes moved to me. "I didn't tell him," he explained, stating the obvious as he moved to scoop Mad out of my arms with an ease I was shocked by. It seemed they'd had a good day.

"When were you two...? How? What the fuck?" Sal barked again in distress. If not for the circumstances, I might have laughed.

"When you went to New York for your grandfather's funeral," Axel spoke up and I was glad he did because I was certainly in no hurry to. "I followed you, had your back even though you didn't know it. After you left, Soph and I well...we... This isn't your business," he growled with impatience. "The short version is we met, had a thing. I fucked it up but it resulted in this guy." He cocked his head down toward Maddox who was drooling like a champ.

"So that whole time she was in Hawthorne you'd already known her. Did you know she was pregnant?" Sal demanded, his eyes wide and shining with confusion and anger.

"Hell, no!" Axel shook his head. "You think had I known that I would have acted like such a jackass? That I would have let her out of my sight? No, I'm guessing your fucked-up parents did something. We haven't gotten into those details, but something made her scared enough to run," he said with halted speech, his emotion such that I moved to take Maddox from him.

Sal's dark gaze swung to mine, leveling me with the pain I saw reflected there. "How could you not have told me?"

"I had every intention to," I rasped, watching him with wide eyes, guilt and apprehension rolling off me in waves. "I ran out of time."

"All right, let's lighten this shit up. Jesus," Wes broke in, coming to give me a one-armed hug. "Who brought the beer?"

"Uh, what exactly is everyone doing here?" I asked hesitantly. "Not that I'm not thrilled to see you but…"

"We figured if you didn't feel safe coming home, we'd bring home to you," Connie grinned, moving in to hug me. "Axel got a head start as soon as Henry told Cole he'd seen you. But we were right behind him."

So it had been Henry. I figured as much.

"But, I…I don't know what to say," I stammered lamely, overwhelmed with how much trouble they'd gone to, with how good they were to me.

"Say you'll finally open up. Say you'll trust us," she pleaded with quiet intensity.

"I always trusted you," I assured her. "It was never about that."

She squeezed me briefly before stepping back. "Welp, my man's right. Let's lighten things up a bit. Where're we eatin'? I'm starved." She winked at me.

I could have kissed her for taking some of the heat off me.

Not half an hour later, we sat in the back room at Giovanni's. Dwayne nearly had a heart attack when we'd all paraded in.

"If I'd known you had access to so many beautiful men,

I would have camped out at your place!" he exclaimed after we were settled.

I gave him what I knew was a stiff smile. Even Dwayne couldn't break my worried mood. I wanted to demand an explanation of what would happen next. What did there being here mean?

"Let's order," I suggested instead, handing Mad a plastic spoon to chew on while we waited.

"How is it that you're so thin having a six-month-old?" Scarlet accused with a smile as she scooped out some baby food for Gracie.

"I can feed her, babe," Cole offered, taking the jar from her and delivering a swift kiss on his wife's cheek.

"She's probably too busy to eat," Connie put in, throwing me a wink.

I shrugged and offered her a shy smile, trying to ignore the tension I noticed in Axel's posture at Connie's flippant remark.

Cole shot me an appraising look, his expression guarded and I knew I was far from being out of hot water with him. I didn't know Cole well, but as Vice President of the Knights' MC, I knew he was not a man you messed with. He was also kind and the most devoted husband and father I'd ever seen. My gaze swung to Sal, sitting at the other end of the table, the anger rolling off him as Kat spoke in his ear. I knew she was trying to calm him down. He hadn't said a word to me or to Axel since we'd left the apartment.

My stomach ached knowing I'd caused all this hurt, all this anger. I couldn't eat a bite of my delicious-looking meal when it came. I was so overcome with worry that I felt sick. "Would you mind feeding Maddox for a few minutes?" I asked Axel who sat to my right.

"Yeah, you all right?" he asked, his tone concerned but distant.

I nodded and scooted my chair back, beelining for the bathroom as the tears escaped their prison and fell in an unrelenting onslaught.

I sobbed as quietly as possible in the bathroom, trying unsuccessfully to pull myself together, wiping my face and taking breath after breath, each as shaky as the last.

When a swift knock sounded followed by the door swinging open, I looked up in surprise as Sal strode in.

"You hate me," I rasped in despair and he surprised me by pulling me into a hug, holding the back of my head as I sobbed into his chest.

"I don't hate you, Soph. I'm just pissed you kept all this from me. Why?" he demanded, his chin resting on my head.

I hiccupped and wiped my eyes. "I didn't tell you about Axel because you were so adverse to him spending time with me at all. I wanted to figure out what was between us, if anything, before I told you about him or the baby," I explained. It was a weak excuse but it was the truth. "I always intended to tell you. I thought I had time. It was never my intention to leave Hawthorne. Regardless of what happened with Axel, I was planning to stay if you'd have me." I saw his expression soften some and knew he believed me. "Please don't be mad at Axel. He never wronged me. He just didn't want me." I shook my head.

He sighed in resignation. "I don't think that's true, Soph. I've known for a long time there was something between you two. It was obvious to everyone. I just had no idea you had any type of history."

"I wouldn't call it history," I muttered. "More like one night he regretted."

Sal pulled me away from him. "That's between you and him. But based on how he's been since you left, I don't think that's true either. He and I will work our shit out," he replied tensely. "Don't worry about that. As long as he does right by you and my nephew, we'll be straight. What I want to know is why you left and I want to know right now."

Sal never did beat around the bush.

"I'm afraid of what you'll do," I admitted, looking off to the side.

"You should be," he replied without hesitation.

"Not helping," I muttered.

The bathroom door swung open followed by a girl who gasped in surprise at seeing us in there. "Sorry," I apologized hurriedly. "We were just leaving. It's all yours," I told her, pushing through the door with Sal at my heels.

"Soph, you're not getting out of this," he warned.

I sighed. "I know but can we not have this conversation in a bathroom?"

He looked down at me and nodded once, throwing an arm over my shoulder as we walked back out to our table. I could have cried again with relief at knowing even though I still had a long road ahead with Sal, we'd be okay. He'd forgive me. Eventually.

He wasn't the one I was really worried about.

Axel took in my expression when I returned to my seat. "Okay?" he asked gruffly.

I nodded simply and offered him a wan smile.

After dinner, everyone went back to their hotel rooms except for Sal and Kat who came back to my apartment.

Kat was helping me put Maddox to bed while Axel and Sal exchanged words in the parking lot. Well, I hoped it was just words anyway.

I'd moved Mad's small crib into my room for the night so we could sit in the living room and talk. The very idea of that talk was giving me yet another stomachache.

"He's so beautiful, Soph," she smiled as she cradled my son in her arms.

"Thanks," I grinned, my heart swelling with being able to share him with the people I loved.

"He and Gracie, and our little peanut, will all be so close in age," she smiled fondly, rubbing her belly.

Tears filled my eyes as my heart twisted. My emotions warred with wanting my son to grow up around so many people who loved him and not being willing to put those I loved at risk.

"We're gonna figure it out, Soph," Kat soothed, observing my internal turmoil.

I bit my lip, hoping desperately she was right as I placed Mad in his crib.

Kat and I were getting situated on the couch when the guys returned, both looking unscathed, thank God.

Axel dipped into the fridge, pulling out three beers for Sal, himself and me. I wasn't sure where they'd come from, but I took mine gratefully.

I saw him scan the room. "I put Maddox in my room," I explained.

"You moved the crib by yourself?" He seemed affronted.

"It's small," I shrugged. I was so used to doing everything by myself it hadn't even occurred to me to ask for his help.

"How have you done this by yourself?" Kat marveled, picking up on my line of thinking.

I shrugged, embarrassed at the attention as they looked to me. "I had some cash I'd taken out of my trust fund before it got cut off. That got me through until I could start working," I explained softly.

"Your trust fund got cut off?" Sal demanded, looking angry and perplexed. "I don't see how they could do that, Soph. Wasn't that trust set up for you by Pop?" he asked, referring to our grandfather.

I nodded. "I don't understand it either, but when Mom and Dad found out I was pregnant, they threatened to cut if off if I didn't follow their orders."

"Which were?" Sal pressed.

I looked over at Axel finding his expression grim as he waited for me to continue.

"They wanted me to get rid of 'it'" as they said. They were horrified I'd sullied my 'pristine' reputation. They said no one would want me," I murmured, looking down at my hands. "They already had me virtually married off to some senator's son. I'd never even met him." I laughed without humor. "So I took as much cash as I could from my fund and I was on the first bus to Hawthorne," I explained.

"Fuck," Axel clipped, his head in his hands. "How could you not have told me?"

"I needed to know where we stood first," I explained quietly. "If I told you about the baby right away, I know you would have done the right thing. That might have included being with me and I didn't want to always wonder if you were with me out of obligation. So I decided to wait."

Out of everything I'd done, I knew that was the most selfish but I just couldn't stand the thought that I'd always wonder if he really wanted me. I didn't want my child to grow up with two parents in a loveless relationship. I'd grown up with it and I wouldn't make my child do the same.

I sipped my drink and pushed on, ready to get it all out. "When it seemed like there wasn't going to be anything between us, I knew I had to tell you. It was so hard. I kept wimping out." I wrinkled my nose and pushed on despite Axel's growl. "But I knew I'd start to show soon and every day I told myself it would be the day. I'm sorry. I waited too long."

"You were planning to stay?" he asked, seeming surprised.

I nodded. "If you wanted to be in the baby's life, I wanted him to have both parents, despite what our circumstances might be."

"Why did you leave?" Axel demanded.

I rubbed my temple. "My parents were incensed that I'd left. That I'd run to Sal. I think they thought cutting off my trust fund would bring me straight home. They were horrified I'd let my child be raised by 'low-lives.' When nothing they'd said after a month was working to get me home, they turned to threats," I whispered as every set of eyes in the room narrowed.

"The hang-ups?" Axel demanded. He'd been with me a few times when my father had tried to reach me.

"He only hung up when you answered. Every other time, he had plenty to say," I assured him dryly.

I sighed, knowing I needed to continue but I was wrung out. In one sense, it was liberating to get it all out but it was exhausting at the same time.

"When he called that last time," I swallowed against

the sudden lump in my throat, "he had information on the club. He swore he could send every single member to prison." I pushed past the sudden, overwhelming tension in the room. "He knew your grandmother was in a nursing home," I rasped, turning my eyes to Axel. "He said he could cut off funding immediately."

I looked down at my hands, my knuckles white around the bottle I held.

"He told me if I stayed, he'd make sure my child's father rotted in jail. That if I went through with it and had the baby, that they'd t-take him from me." Tears fell in earnest as I continued. "I never knew he could be so evil." I sucked in a ragged breath. "So I told him I'd leave town and that I'd get rid of the baby if he'd leave everyone alone. The night I left, I bought a new phone, used a different last name and tried not to look back." I expelled a breath, leaning back against the couch cushions, relieved to have it out.

"Fuck, Sophie," Sal grunted, at a loss for words.

"I believed him, Sal. I still do. You guys should go back to Hawthorne and pretend you never saw me."

"Like hell," Axel growled, rising to pace the room. "First of all, I doubt he has jack shit on any of us," he bit out. "We run the club clean, except when we don't, and if any motherfucker I've jacked up has something to say, then it's their fucking funeral," he growled. "As for my gran; he cuts off funding, the club will pay for it. I don't give a fuck. What I care about is that your parents are twisted enough to pull this kind of shit. I want you back in Hawthorne where I can take care of you. I don't like that you've been alone this whole time. I want you with us where nothing can touch you or Maddox," he decreed. "No one threatens my family."

I felt my eyes widen at the 'his family' part.

"He's right, Soph," Sal spoke up as Kat put a steadying hand on his back. She was always so good in these situations. So calming for my brother. "I understand why they scared you. But even if they had anything, I'm going to dig up enough shit to bury them both." His eyes glowed with emotion as he spoke. He put a hand on my knee and squeezed briefly. "Come home. You belong with us."

Tears once again filled my eyes. Could that really be true? Could we really go back?

"I'm so sorry, for everything," my voice cracked.

"You were trying to protect us and Maddox. I get it," Sal replied. "But, Soph, no more lies. No more secrets, yeah?"

"Yeah," I sighed.

"All right, we gotta jet. Kat's tired," he spoke up, and for the first time, I noticed she looked exhausted.

I smiled at her sympathetically, remembering those days well.

"We're flying out tomorrow. Let's get with Cole in the morning before we leave." Sal shot a look at Axel.

"Right," Axel agreed.

"It's gonna be okay, Soph," Kat whispered in my ear, giving me a reassuring squeeze. "Love you, sis."

"Me, too." I squeezed her back.

Then they were gone, and I was left alone with Axel.

"I'm kind of talked out," I warned when I got a look at his pensive expression.

"There's just one thing I need to get straight," he replied, sitting close to me on the couch.

Great. I had a feeling I wasn't going to like that 'one

thing' whatever it was.

"When you said you didn't think there was going to be a you and me, what the fuck did that mean?" he demanded.

Exasperated, I sighed, "Axel, what else would I have thought? We slept together and you were freaked." I winced at the memory.

"You should have told me it was your first time!" he growled. "Christ, Soph, you deserved so much better than me. You're so innocent and sweet and you're my buddy's sister. I had no business going there. None." He shook his head.

"Yeah, well, you did," I grumbled.

"You think I forgot? That night, it's been with me ever since. I can still smell you. Still feel the softness of your skin. I can still taste you." His eyes turned dark as they swept my face.

Heat blazed across my cheeks as I forced myself to stay calm, outwardly at least.

"Then why? Why didn't you want me when I came to Hawthorne?" I demanded heatedly.

"Not want you? Fuck, I've never wanted anyone more. But I still thought you deserved better. You're younger than me, Soph, and on top of that, you were so damn sheltered. No matter how much I fucking wanted you," he emphasized his words as his eyes lit. "I wasn't sure I could be good for you. You're Sal's only family. He loves you. I knew I couldn't just fuck around with you, so I acted like an ass." He admitted. "But when you disappeared, I was haunted by it, Sophie. Haunted." His voice grew hoarse with his declaration. "I knew I may not deserve you, but it doesn't change the fact that you're mine. That's why I came here. I came for you. The second Henry found you, I was on the first flight out. Maddox is just a big, unexpected bonus." He looked over at me, his eyes shining with sincerity.

Well, hell, that just about rocked my world. But I couldn't trust it – not yet.

Overwhelmed, I replied quietly, "This is all just so much to take in. I'm still so worried, and things with you and me…they were always so confusing," I sighed.

"I get it. You'll see it with time." He shrugged as though this were a fact not to be disputed. "And during that time, you and Mad are gonna be under my roof."

"Uh, what?"

"We're on a flight day after tomorrow. We can have your shit shipped out. Anything you need in the interim, I'll buy you. We've wasted too much time. Mad needs me and whether or not you know it yet, so do you."

Apparently, we'd moved into full Alpha territory with a capital A embossed in bright red letters.

"I have a job here!" I huffed. "An apartment. Jill!" I shook my head, rising from the couch to glare down at him. "I can't just abandon my responsibilities and leave." I pointed an accusing finger at him. "I'm not that same scared girl you knew. I spent my life under my parents' thumb, and for the past year, I've called the shots. I've been in charge of my own destiny," I shot out. "I'm not going to start taking orders."

"I hear you, baby," he allowed with a nod, watching as I stood over him with my hands on my hips, trying hard to not let the endearment turn me to mush. "Judging by all that finger pointin', this is a sore subject," he noted wryly. "But if your parents weren't still pulling the strings, you wouldn't be here in the first place."

Oh, hell, he was right. Dammit!

"The way I see it, the way to be free of them is to live the life you wanted all along and I'll be damned if that's not with me."

"I have to go to bed," I blurted. I was in no form to go toe-to-toe with him, though I doubted a little sleep would change that much.

He chuckled, his mood lightening. "All right, baby. I'll help you get packed up in the morning." He shrugged as though the subject was closed.

I groaned in frustration at his assumption that he'd win this argument, and stomped off to bed.

Chapter Five

"You're quiet," Axel observed as we began our descent into Reno. He'd held Maddox for nearly the entire flight, leaving me my space to gaze out the window and hope like hell I was doing the right thing.

The decision to leave Texas hadn't been as easy as I would have imagined. Though I never loved the place, I'd created a life there, albeit an isolated one, and it had been Maddox's only home.

Plus I was downright terrified my parents would carry out their threats, despite Axel's constant reassurances.

Leaving Jill had been the hardest. She was my closest girlfriend and I owed her so much. The guilt was eating at me. I kept thinking about having to say goodbye to her.

"Your life has been on hold," she said firmly as we'd both wiped our eyes when I'd taken Mad over to say goodbye. *"I've always seen that in you. It's time to start living."*

I nodded and squeezed her hard.

"When that man is in the room, your eyes light up like I've never seen," she grinned. *"I see good things."* She gave me an assuring wink.

"We'll see." I rolled my eyes. The state of Axel and me was

still far from clear. "*When Tim goes out of town again, will you come visit?*" *I asked hopefully.*

"*Sure,*" *she agreed with the brittle smile I was used to seeing when her husband was mentioned.*

I would make sure she kept that agreement, planning on scraping enough money together to fly her and Mason out.

I was so lost in thought, I didn't realize Axel had been speaking to me.

"Soph?" he said, his tone concerned as he pulled me from my thoughts.

"I'm fine," I assured him, popping a pacifier in Mad's mouth so the landing wouldn't hurt his ears.

I watched the desert from below, the sun and landscape I'd missed so much welcoming me home.

"What a beautiful little boy!" an older woman cooed as we stood waiting to deplane.

"Thank you," I responded, holding Mad as Axel gathered up our things. It was still so odd to have someone else help with Mad and with life in general. Axel handled everything with my landlord while I'd dealt with giving notice at work. Axel made my sudden departure as easy as he could on me; though no one could have stopped Dwayne's temper tantrum and subsequent meltdown.

A part of me was afraid of becoming reliant on the help, as though it could all just suddenly disappear.

"Look at that. He has his daddy's eyes." She smiled.

I met Axel's heated gaze for a moment, his emotion boiling just below the surface. He liked that people knew instantly that Mad was his. A lot. I returned her smile and followed the rest of the passengers off the small airplane.

We gathered up the three large suitcases, portable crib

and car seat we'd checked. When it came down to it, Mad and I didn't have many belongings. The apartment had come furnished and I'd bought very little, trying to keep a tight budget.

"Ready?" he asked, looking down at me.

"Yep," I muttered not sure at all if I meant it.

Maddox fell asleep in the back of Axel's truck as we drove the hour to his place just outside of Hawthorne. I'd never even been there, and agreeing to live there with my baby might have been one of the crazier things I'd done.

Aside from the whole getting knocked up by a biker, getting my trust fund cut off and going the single working-mother route for the past year business.

Yeah, aside from all that.

We drove farther outside of town than I would have expected and into the mountains, the landscape growing more rugged with a thick layer of pine lining the road on either side.

"I didn't realize you lived in the boons."

"I like the space and the quiet." He shrugged, glancing at me with as close to a shy grin as I'd ever seen on him. If possible, it made him more handsome.

We pulled down an unpaved road to a house I instantly loved.

It looked like a contemporary cabin, but large with a welcoming wrap-around porch. It had a tin roof, practical for snow in the winter and huge windows lining the majority of the home.

"It's beautiful," I sighed as he cut the engine. The quiet was deafening for a moment as I tried to absorb the fact that this was home, for now at least.

He looked over at me, searching my face. "Glad you

like it," he replied after a long moment. Something about his tone made me realize how important that was to him. "He's out," he commented, his tone lightening as he tilted his head in Mad's direction.

I looked back and smiled tenderly at my son. "It's been a big day. I bet he'll sleep a while longer if we carry him inside and put him someplace quiet."

Axel nodded, moving to the back and carrying our son inside.

The interior was just as beautiful as the outside. We walked into a great room with vaulted ceilings and floor-to-ceiling windows that looked out to the wilderness beyond. The kitchen was dated but practical with what looked like lots of storage.

He led me down a hall to the left, pointing out an office, a guestroom and a master at the end.

He set Mad down in the master, still sleeping peacefully in his car seat and shut the door quietly.

"What were you thinking the sleeping arrangements would be?" I asked as we wandered back out to the living room. I collapsed on one of the two sofas in the large room. Both were worn, a bit shabby even, but so comfortable I never wanted to get up.

He shrugged. "I can easily move my office into the mudroom downstairs. We can turn the office into his nursery. As for you," he continued, his voice dropping an octave. "You can sleep in the guestroom – until you're ready to move into my room."

I fought the panic that threatened to overtake me. "This is all moving really fast." I swallowed audibly as his eyes narrowed. "For now, can we just put Mad's crib in the office and I'll crash in the guestroom?"

He eyed me intently for a few beats. "For now," he allowed and I knew it cost him.

I laid my head back against the couch looking up at the ceiling, relieved he wasn't going to push further.

"When did you move here?"

"This was my granddad's place. Mad's namesake," he added. "He left it to me and Ry in his will," he continued, referring to his younger brother who was also a member of the Knights. "When he died, Gran was already in a home. I bought Ry out; he didn't want to be this far from town. He helped me with a lot of the updates. We broke down a lot of the walls, opened the place up, and added a hell of a lot more windows. All kinds of shit." He shrugged. "That was close to five years ago now."

"It looks beautiful," I told him sincerely. "It's really far from town," I added absently, though I didn't mind it. Once I moved to Hawthorne, I soon realized I liked the small town. I loved the desert juxtaposed with the mountains. I loved that the heat was dry, not bogged down with humidity like New York and God, Dallas. There hadn't been anything like that heat.

"We'll get you a car." He shrugged.

"I still don't know how to drive," I admitted, feeling my cheeks heat.

His brows rose in surprise. "Seriously?"

I looked down at the fraying seam of the sofa. "Seriously. Will you teach me?" Though I liked the scenery, I had no desire to be stranded in the mountains or beholden to Axel to get me around all the time.

A look of possession passed over his features before he nodded. "You bet," he agreed.

*****

Maddox fussed all night. It was 2 a.m. and I was ducking into the office for the fifth time.

Axel was already there. I stopped short, watching as his shirtless form held our boy, murmuring to him in his deep baritone voice.

There was something about that moment; such tenderness pooling from this formidable man. A man who hadn't known he had a son a week ago yet accepted him, seemed to have fallen in love with him as instantly as I had.

"He's never slept anywhere else," I explained with a whisper, moving to stroke my hand over his soft head of hair. "I think I'll just see if he'll sleep with me," I added.

"Come on, my bed's bigger," he murmured.

"But—" I tried to protest.

He cut me off. "He'll feel better if we're both there."

Part of me wanted to argue further but mostly I wanted to give him this – the confidence to feel he could comfort our baby. I was touched he wanted to try.

So it ended up that we shared Axel's huge king-sized bed with Maddox stretched out and sleeping peacefully between us.

Axel and I shared a look, gazing at each other from opposite sides of the bed as his large hand lay sprawled gently over our son's belly.

I smiled at him, the first true smile I'd had in as long as I could remember. The kind that started from the inside and shone outward like a beacon.

"There it is," he rasped, his eyes shining with joy.

"What?" I asked quietly.

"My light," he replied simply.

We spent the next few days settling in. Maddox started sleeping more peacefully in his new room, which meant

I was back to the guest room much to Axel's very clear displeasure. I got to work on his home that, though more organized than I would have expected, was lacking in essentials. He needed everything from new towels to pots and pans.

"You ever miss it?" he asked as we meandered through Target with Mad noisily chewing a teething cracker in the cart. Axel had been determined to come with us and I was still trying to get used to seeing this intimidating looking man casually draped over the bright red cart as we strolled the aisles.

"What?" I asked absently.

"The money." He shrugged, surprising me with his line of thinking.

"Not really," I replied and he cocked a brow at my response as though he didn't believe me. "It wasn't like I could do anything with it that I really wanted to anyway," I explained. "I couldn't even buy the clothes I wanted, listen to the music I would have, or experiment with well… anything. In the end, it was all just another way for them to try to control me. So now I shop here instead of Nieman Marcus." I shrugged as I ran my hands over some throw pillows absently. "At least I get to pick what I like without someone else defining that for me."

"So you don't miss any of it?" he pressed.

I sighed. "I mean, sure, if I really think about it, I miss having someone cook for me since I'm crap at it." I smiled though I really shouldn't be. My cooking was deadly as I'd discovered over the last year. Thank God I'd just been cooking for myself and once for Jill. After that attempt, she always just had me over. "I miss my bathtub; it was killer. But I guess as far as possessions go, I still regret leaving my grandmother's necklace. She gave it to me when I turned fifteen. It was beautiful and one of the few sentimental things I owned. But I couldn't find it in my rush to leave." I bit my lip and looked away from his penetrating gaze. "Other than that it's all just stuff." I shrugged. "Do you need dish cloths?" I asked, ready to change the subject.

He looked at me for a moment longer before he nodded. "Yeah, babe, we probably do." He made sure to emphasize the 'we' as I threw a few into the cart.

Chapter Six

"I've got somewhere to take you two," he stated after loading everything into the back of the truck.

I turned to him in surprise. I assumed we'd be headed back to his place. Maddox was going to need a nap soon.

It was as though he knew I was considering protesting when he turned to look at me. "It's important." There was a weighted silence as his jaw flexed. "To me," he added gruffly.

That was all he needed to say. "Okay," I nodded. It was early yet, hopefully Mad would hang in a while longer.

We drove north for a few miles, my curiosity growing though I held back from asking any questions. He'd share when he was ready. He always allowed me that space and I'd give the same to him.

The answer was soon clear without my having to ask.

When we pulled into the Oakcrest Nursing Home and parked, he sighed. "She has good days and bad days," he shared, looking straight ahead and rubbing a hand over his beard. "But I'm hoping today's a good day. Regardless, I want her to meet Maddox – and you."

I knew little about Axel's family but I did know

through passing conversations that his grandma and late grandfather had been pivotal for him and Ry growing up.

I was moved that he was so intent on introducing us.

I reached over, tentatively placing a hand on his forearm. "We'd like to meet her, too," I assured him softly.

He threw me a rueful smile and cut the engine.

The smell hit me first – like old food and disinfectant. I fought the urge to wrinkle my nose against it and instead held Maddox closer. As I tried to keep up with Axel's long strides down the hall, I noted that although outdated, the facility looked clean and well cared for.

"She's in here," he nodded, indicating an open door to the right.

Axel's grandmother was sitting up in a bed that nearly swallowed her small frame. She looked over at us when we walked in, her face blank for a few moments before her expression warmed.

"My boy," she smiled, holding her hands out. Axel stooped down, allowing her to cup his face. "I'll never get used to this beard," she tisked.

"Had it ten years, Gran," he chuckled, stepping back and looking over at me.

"You've brought company," she nodded, looking over at Mad and me curiously.

Axel brought his arm up putting it around my shoulders and bringing us closer. "I did, very important company," he told her. "Gran, this is Sophie, my girl," he explained and my heart fluttered. "Sophie, this is my gran, Sybil."

I gave her a little wave.

"And this is our son – Maddox."

For a moment, she didn't react and I braced for a variety of reactions. I hoped she didn't have a heart condition because that was quite a ball to drop. Before I could grow too concerned, a slow smile spread across her face.

"Bring that baby closer so my old eyes can see him," she beckoned. Axel lifted him from my arms and brought him closer.

"Aren't you beautiful," she crooned to him, her hand moving over his chubby cheek. "I see your grandfather so clearly," she stated, her voice full of wonder as she looked up at Axel. "Don't you?"

He nodded once, his jaw flexing. I bit back tears at how moved he clearly was.

"And you, beautiful girl, let me see you." She raised a hand toward me. I moved closer, offering a tentative smile. "Well, aren't you a looker," she grinned, cupping my cheeks the way she'd done Axel's.

"Thank you," I murmured. "It's great to meet you, Sybil."

"It's wonderful to meet you; though, you're giving an old lady quite the surprise!" she chortled.

Axel cleared his throat. "It's a long story, Gran," he responded.

That was one way of putting it.

She waved her hand. "I'm sure. All I care about is spending time with my great grandchild. Will you bring him on your visits?" she asked Axel.

I wondered how often he came here. He'd never mentioned it.

"Sure, Gran," he agreed, sitting Maddox on the bed so he could play with the remote control.

"Maddox," she whispered reverently, her eyes moving over Mad though I could tell her thoughts were elsewhere. "He would have loved to meet this baby," she sighed.

"I know," Axel agreed.

We stayed until Maddox made it known that he was done. It always amazed me how quickly his good mood could take a turn toward a full-blown meltdown.

"We'll come back soon," Axel assured her as we gathered our things.

"Good," she clapped her hands together in glee as he leaned down to kiss her cheek. "You too, Sophie, or come back without these boys so I can get the full story," she winked.

I blushed. "Okay."

"Love you, boy," she told Axel.

"Me, too," he returned, hoisting Maddox up into his arms and leading us out of the room.

Maddox fell asleep in the truck on the drive back to Axel's. I knew I shouldn't bombard him with questions so I cut my thousand questions down to a few.

"Why is she in a home?" I asked, looking over at him as he watched the road ahead.

He sighed. "She started forgetting things, leaving the stove on, shit like that. It just wasn't safe. Ry and I felt like shit putting her in a home but she actually seems to like it. She has friends, so when she's having a good day, she plays cards with them. The nurses love her," he smiled.

"I bet," I was already in love with her myself. "So that was a good day I take it?"

"Yeah," he nodded, sounding relieved. "Even on bad days she still knows who I am, but she doesn't always remember the year or that my granddad's gone. She gets confused and agitated. It's not easy."

"I'm sure it's not," I agreed as we began ascending the mountain.

"How often do you visit her?"

He shrugged. "Ry and I trade off weeks, but when I have time, I go every week." His jaw ticked and I could tell the conversation was making him agitated. "When we get back, I'll help you unload all this shit and then I gotta make some calls," he added, indicating the subject was closed. For now.

******

Later that day, Axel dropped me and Mad off at Scarlet and Cole's so he could take care of some 'club shit' as he called it.

"So how's it going with Axel?" Scarlet asked as we sipped beers in her living room, watching Mad and Gracie get acquainted. So far, that acquaintance had consisted of Gracie toddling over and snatching any toy Maddox seemed interested in.

I wrinkled my nose and she laughed, her green eyes shining. "I don't know, good I guess?"

"Why is that a question?" she laughed.

"He's been amazing with Mad. He's such a natural dad." I looked over at Maddox and smiled, so grateful every day that my son would have a father who loved him in his life. "Living together has been okay. It's just a little awkward sometimes," I admitted.

"Awkward how?" she asked, rising to let their giant bullmastiff, Chief, in from outside.

"Well, he's made it clear he wants to give things a shot. He speaks about it like it's a forgone conclusion," I grumbled. "He even took Maddox and me to meet his gran today. But I don't know if I'm ready for all of this! It's all been so sudden and he certainly didn't seem to want me when I came to town before. I still don't quite believe the intense change of direction, how sure he is about us. So for now, we spend a bunch of time together but we're also kind of skirting around each other," I tried to explain.

"Sometimes it takes something really big for our pig-headed men to understand how they feel about things." She rolled her eyes. "It was that way for Sal, you know? He had to leave to gain perspective. For Axel, it was your leaving that did it. And, honey, trust me, it did it. That man was not the same when you left." She shook her head.

"Really?" I gasped with surprise. I'd heard this in so many words from him, but somehow, hearing it from her made it really sink in.

"Really. You want my advice? Give it a shot, Soph. You guys have a baby together. I think you owe it to yourselves and that little man over there." She cocked her head toward Mad.

"I hear you," I agreed taking a sip of my drink.

"I'm so glad you're here. We all missed you," she added quietly.

"Me, too. I'm just hoping that giant shoe I feel every day doesn't actually drop." I winced, sharing the fear that kept me up every night.

She squeezed my thigh briefly and empathized, "God, I know how that feels. But what was your other option? Raising Maddox alone forever? That's no life for you or him." She shook her head. "You can't live off the grid forever. Now you've got all of us at your front and your back, and Mad can have his daddy."

"You're right," I agreed, feeling a weight I hadn't known was there lift a little bit.

"You can have his daddy, too," she winked before

she seemed to ponder something. "Will you tell me what happened between you two…before? I have to confess, I'm sort of dying of curiosity."

I blushed. "I'm sure you're not the only one."

"True," she laughed. "I'll keep the details to myself if you're willing to share," she swore with wide, expectant eyes.

I sighed and tipped my head back to the ceiling, searching for a place to start. The beginning was as good a place as any. "I was sitting out on my aunt's front steps; it was my grandfather's memorial service," I began, deciding I might as well tell someone. I relived the memory in my head so many times. "I probably wasn't supposed to even see him. Sal and Kat had left and my mother came out to berate me." I winced. "Instead of letting me grieve, she was on my case about my outfit, about how I hadn't introduced myself to one of my father's colleagues. The criticism seemed to go on and on. It was awful. It had already been such an emotional day with my grandfather's funeral and then seeing Sal and meeting Kat…" I trailed off, lost in thought. "Axel came up out of nowhere. My savior," I laughed, though I meant every word. "He told my mother off, right there on the spot. Told her to go take that rod up her ass right back into the house and learn how to talk to her daughter." I grinned, remembering the moment like it was yesterday. "He introduced himself as Sal's buddy, said he'd been late to the service though I know now Sal wasn't even supposed to know he was there at all. He asked me to go out for a drink." I watched as Maddox squealed at Gracie. "Normally, I would have never done that – gone out with a complete stranger, but after the day I'd had, I wanted to do something that wasn't me and he had been so protective and was gorgeous," I sighed wistfully.

"You were a goner," Scarlet surmised.

"Completely," I agreed.

"We had a few drinks. I'd never experienced chemistry like we had. Not before or after him." I shook my head. "It was so powerful. I just got caught up in it." I shrugged, playing with the fringes of their throw pillow. "I still can't believe I went back to his hotel. I've never done anything like that. There was just something about him – about us together that I couldn't deny. It was so not me," I laughed.

"Been there." She nodded, confirming why she was the right person to share this with. Scarlet had a way of identifying with you on such a genuine basis.

"When we started fooling around…" I trailed off, my cheeks heating. "He said once how we should stop since I was Sal's little sister. He seemed to feel guilty."

I thought back to that moment where indecision had suddenly clouded his expression. I couldn't explain the feeling, but despite being mere strangers, I'd needed him more than my next breath. For one night, I found my true self. He'd brought that out in me.

I'd been fun.

I'd been free.

In the brief time we spent together, it was as though I broke out of a suffocating cocoon. I needed him to take me – to make me fly.

"I convinced him there was no need to stop."

"You sly minx. You seduced him!" Scarlet hooted.

Had I?

"Maybe a bit," I admitted with a smothered grin. "But, well, I hadn't told him it was my first time." I blushed crimson.

"Oh, shit," Scarlet exclaimed.

"Yeah, he, uh…well, he kind of freaked. I should have told him." I bit my lip.

"Then what happened?" she prodded, her green eyes wide with curiosity.

"I could tell he was freaked. It was so awkward," I groaned. "It was pretty clear he regretted it, so I didn't stay the night with him. I left."

"So let me get this straight; you basically coerced him into sleeping with you and then bailed on him?" she squeaked.

I hadn't really thought about it quite like that.

"I guess," I muttered.

"So when you came back to town, he didn't know what the hell to do with you, girl." She continued to grin as though our situation was the most entertaining news she'd heard in a long time – hell, maybe it was.

I hung my head in my hands. "God, I really have no business being outside in the world," I groaned.

She reached over to me, squeezing my arm. "Seems like it's all working out okay, honey." She smiled warmly.

"Yeah," I agreed.

I heard the rumble of Axel's truck and turned my head toward the sound. I had to admit, I missed the sound of his bike. Since we had Maddox, most of the time the truck had become his main source of transportation.

I'd ridden the bike a few times with him and it had been a thrill to wrap myself around him as the wind whipped through my hair.

When he walked in, I felt that familiar flutter I always felt when it came to him. He was wearing his standard Levis and a black t-shirt under his cut. He swept his brown hair from his face as his expressive eyes met mine.

"Hi," I murmured with a shy smile.

"Hi," he replied, his gaze sweeping over my face, landing a beat longer on my lips. I could feel my face heat again and I licked them involuntarily, watching his eyes turn dark. He moved through the room to Maddox, lifting him up in his strong arms.

The sound of a bike rumbling to a stop made Gracie's face light up.

"Daddy," Scarlet grinned to her.

Cole walked in a moment later to grins from both the ladies in his life. He delivered a kiss to his wife and scooped his squealing daughter up in his arms.

I rose up off the couch, gathering the diaper bag and any stray toys we'd left lying around. "We'll see you soon." I hugged Scar in parting.

"You'll see me the day after tomorrow along with everyone else," she informed me.

"What?" I asked.

"The club wanted to welcome you home, Soph," Cole told me, his blue eyes warm on mine.

Sal and Axel both assured me that the reasons why I'd left had been shared and were understood, respected even, by the Knights. It showed in the much warmer way Cole treated me since I'd returned to town.

"Wow, okay," I stuttered, beyond moved at the gesture. I looked to Axel with a question in my eyes. He hadn't mentioned this.

"Let's get you two home," he said by way of answer.

"Why didn't you say anything?" I asked quietly as he backed out of their driveway and gunned the gas, headed for the highway.

He shrugged. "I wanted it to come from Scar. Figured that way you wouldn't say no," he chuckled. "You seem to argue with me about everything."

"Good play," I replied dryly and he laughed harder, reaching over and putting his large hand over mine. I turned it over, palm up and laced his fingers with mine.

Electricity zinged down my spine as I felt his gaze on me. He was looking over at me with surprise as I turned to meet his gaze.

He grinned. The man was beautiful on any occasion, but when he smiled, he was breathtaking. "She's gettin' it," he muttered to himself, his eyes turning back to the road.

"Yeah," I admitted. "She is."

I put Maddox to bed and Axel and I sat out on his large back deck eating a casual dinner and sipping beers.

"It's beautiful here," I sighed, loving the smell of the pine trees, the orchestra of crickets and the occasional owl.

"Yeah," he agreed. "Scar offered to babysit." His pose was casual as his boots rested on the railing, crossed at the ankle.

"Oh?" I asked, my heart beating a little harder in my chest.

"Yeah, I want to take you out to dinner."

"Like a date?" I asked incredulously. "Ax, we have a kid together. I think we're past the first date."

"Well, it can be our second date then," he replied easily.

"All right, second date," I clinked his bottle with mine.

I slinked off to bed like I had since we'd been staying with him. I was still so nervous about taking things to a romantic level between us. I couldn't place where the anxiety came from. Lack of experience? Fear of rejection? Whatever it was, I was like a freaking skittish cat when it came to being close to him.

"Night, baby," I heard him call. He knew I was running away from him. He'd allow me this for the time being, but I knew it wouldn't last forever.

When my phone rang with a call from Jill an hour later, I smiled, excited to catch up with her. I'd been reading in bed after having a hard time falling asleep.

"Hi, there," I greeted warmly.

Her reply was full of concern. "Hi, Soph."

I sat up straighter in bed at hearing her worried tone, knowing immediately that something was wrong. "What happened?"

"Some men were here looking for you," she told me.

"What?" I demanded.

"They looked sort of like your friends..." She trailed off. "So at first I thought it was okay."

"What do you mean they looked like my friends?" I asked, confused.

"They looked like bikers. At first I thought maybe they were the same guys who were here last week."

My blood chilled as I tried to understand what the hell was going on.

"They didn't bother you?" I asked, immediately concerned for her safety.

"No – they went straight for your door. Do you know who they were?"

"No idea. Did you see any names on any of them?"

"The Black something or other? At least I think that's what their jackets said."

I knew of the Black Riders through the Knights, but I didn't have any idea why the hell they'd be looking for me.

"Did they take anything?" I asked, my teeth biting at

my lip nervously.

"No, they were in and out really fast. I heard one guy say , 'she isn't here'."

"Shit," I whispered.

"Are you safe?" she asked worriedly.

"Clearly safer than if I had stayed," I sighed. "I'm okay, Jill. Axel's taking good care of us."

"I'm glad. You deserve it," she replied quietly. "Keep me in the loop of what you find out and kiss that baby for me."

"Thanks, I will." I hung up, trying to calm my raging nerves.

I was suddenly frantic to check on Maddox. Though rationally, I knew he was sleeping soundly in his crib, I had to lay eyes on him.

I stood over his crib for an indeterminable amount of time just watching his little chest rise and fall. My mind was racing thinking that we could have still been there and what that could have meant.

When Axel's warm hands gently gripped my upper arms from behind, I jumped about a mile in the air, letting out a squeak of alarm. I turned to him, my eyes wide, hand over my heart. "I didn't hear you," I whispered.

"What are you doing in here? Is he okay?" he asked, his eyes shooting beyond me to the crib.

"He's fine," I whispered, my voice hoarse and before I even thought about it, I was throwing my arms around him, burying my face in his neck. My body shook with emotion as I clung to him.

He scooped me up without another word and carried me into his room, depositing me on the bed and crawling up over me, effectively caging me in. Instead of the posture scaring me, his weight and closeness soothed my raging nerves.

"What is it?" His expression was tight as he peered down into my face.

"Jill called," I explained, looking off to the side.

"Eyes on me," he directed.

I conceded, shifting my gaze to his. "Jill called and told me that men broke into my old place tonight." I swallowed as his body grew noticeably tighter. "The thing is," I continued, looking past his expression which had grown dark, "she thought it was you guys at first. She said they were bikers. I have no idea why another club would be looking for me or how they even found me in the first place. Do you think Henry told anyone else that he saw me?" I asked hesitantly. "I know he wouldn't do anything to put me in harm's way, but maybe he just didn't know to keep that information to himself."

"I don't know what the fuck is going on but I'm sure as hell gonna find out," he growled.

"She said she thought she saw Black something on their jackets. The Black Riders?" I asked my question aloud.

I could feel his muscles go tighter still as he absorbed this information.

"God, we could have still been there." I closed my eyes trying to block out the images that had haunted me since Jill's call. "What if they had taken Mad from me?" I croaked, my eyes filling with tears. "What if—"

"You weren't there," his deep voice cut off my line of thinking as he swept my hair away from my face. "And I'll never let anyone take our boy. I'll never let anyone hurt you," he soothed.

I believed him. He had my back from minute one,

despite all the bombshells I dropped on him.

"Come here, babe," he rumbled, rolling us so he was on his side and I was pulled deep into his body. It was only then I was really aware he was nearly naked, clad only in boxers. Being pressed against his firm chest, smelling his natural woodsy scent was almost enough to bring me out of my state of fear entirely.

I breathed him in, burrowing deeper. I would have crawled inside him if I could have.

"What are we going to do? How is this going to end?" I whispered as his large hand stroked over the dip in my waist and up to the curve of my hip in a rhythmic gesture.

"We aren't going to do anything. " He squeezed my hip for emphasis. "I'm going to take care of this and you're going to trust me to do that."

I pulled away and looked him in the eye. "I do trust you and a year ago I would have turned a blind eye, but our son is involved. I want to know what's going on."

He was silent for a few moments and I braced for his response. "All right, darlin'. But you may not like what I tell you," he warned. "I'm not afraid to use whatever means necessary to get the information I want. Especially if it comes to keeping you and Maddox safe."

"Whatever means necessary?" I asked quietly.

He nodded, his jaw tight. "Violence is a part of my world. You should understand that about me," he explained gruffly. "That means anyone gets out of line, I put them back in it. That means anyone threatens you, I will not fucking hesitate to make them regret it. No one will take you from me. No one," he growled.

"We're here now," I assured him – comforting him as he had me so many times.

"Are you here, Soph?" he demanded quietly. "You're so damn quiet. I can never tell what you're thinkin'. You don't want to touch me except for right now. Is it...was I just too late? Did I lose you even though you're here?" His voice was thick with emotion.

My heart lurched, thinking of what I put him through. What we'd put each other through. Especially with so many unknowns of what was to come, it was never more poignant to me to live in the moment. To let the past go.

I knew words wouldn't appease him.

Actions would.

I kissed his chest by way of answer. I heard his intake of breath and his grip tightened on my hip. "You sure?" he growled as I moved to his neck. "Cause if you go much further—"

"I'm sure," I cut him off, moving up over him and taking his lips. God, how I dreamed of those lips.

He pulled me up so I straddled his muscular frame, his hands grasping my thighs as his mouth opened under mine.

Our tongues tangled as heat flooded my entire body and my heart pounded. Kissing Axel was like nothing else on earth.

His hands moved to the hair at the back of my neck, gripping me like his life depended on it. His erection, hot and insistent at my core pressed against me, and I ground down, unable to hold back, not that either of us wanted that in the first place.

He flipped us suddenly, looming up over me as he pulled my tank top up and over my head, his lips finding my nipples with a laser-like focus.

I sighed, my back arching into his mouth.

I didn't have time to worry about how my body had changed since having Maddox, or that it was only my second time ever. The dim light and the heat of the moment allowed for me to let any reservations go. I wanted to let my body lead well before my head.

He pulled my panties off, moving lower to territory he hadn't explored our first time.

"You're so gorgeous, Sophie. Christ," he murmured in reverence as he swiped along the seam of my core.

I threw my head back on the pillow, a sound I didn't recognize escaping me.

I loved the feeling of his tongue, of his hands gripping my thighs, thighs that quickly began to shake.

"That's right, baby," he rasped in encouragement.

He slipped one finger inside me and I was hurling over the edge, calling out his name, my thighs caging his head, keeping him there as I rode out my orgasm.

After a moment, my legs slackened and I took a few last shuddering breaths. He rose from the bed, shedding the boxers he'd been wearing. I took in his amazing form in the dim light suddenly wishing it was broad daylight.

"Condom," he murmured, pulling it out of the nightstand before he was back between my legs. He kissed me again, poised at my entrance.

"You gonna let me in?" he asked quietly and I knew he meant more than just physically.

I looked up at his gorgeous face. "You were never out," I admitted. "I look at Mad every day and I see you. I see us. I was gone but I never left you. What if this one breaks too?" I whispered nervously.

"Then I guess we're having another baby," he replied without hesitation.

"I'll get on birth control," I replied quickly, shocked at how swiftly and without fear he'd responded.

"That'd be good," he rasped. He made a noise in the back of his throat as he glided through to the hilt, both of us gasping slightly.

"Christ, baby, you feel so good," he muttered, his tone nearly guttural.

I adjusted slightly, trying to accommodate to his size. Then he started to move.

This was so different from our first time, our only other time, where everything had felt like the promise of something hanging on the edge of a precipice. Back then, it had been as though we were afraid to speak. Neither of us made any promises; I hadn't even told him it was my first time.

This time, I knew he was claiming me in a way he couldn't the first time. His mouth was everywhere it could be, his large hands grasping my flesh. Our sweat intermingled as we nearly toppled off the bed. When he loomed over me and I looked into his eyes, I'd never felt so close to another person.

I watched in fascination as the muscles in his arms, his shoulders, and everywhere I could see worked to pleasure me. He put everything he had into loving me. He gave himself to me.

And I wasn't ever giving him back.

When my orgasm began to build, I gripped his backside pulling him deeper, wanting him closer.

He waited until I was already toppling over the edge, pulling him close, before he let out a low groan of relief and completely enveloped me with his large body.

We lay in a sweaty, heaving heap as we came back to

ourselves. He moved us so that I was on top of him as his hand stroked over my back. I didn't want to get up, ever.

"Let's get some sleep," he suggested, moving us further into the bed and pulling the covers over our bodies.

"I can't sleep naked," I squeaked.

He chuckled. "Why the hell not?"

"I don't know. I just can't," I stammered. "What if there's a fire? What if Mad needs me in an hour?"

"Your clothes are five feet away. I want your skin under my hands," he said in a tone that wasn't to be trifled with.

His large hand swept over my breast down to my stomach before he cupped me intimately.

"Okay," I agreed breathlessly.

"Okay." He pulled my back to his front and we fell asleep with his hand between my legs.

I'd never felt so worshipped in my life.

Chapter Seven

The next morning when Mad was babbling and cooing from his crib, Axel got up, threw on his boxers and brought him back into bed with us.

The three of us lay cuddled close and I didn't think I'd ever felt more content.

"We gotta get to the club," Axel announced when Maddox grew restless and clearly wanted food.

"So early?" I wrinkled my brow.

He scoffed, throwing on a t-shirt as I rose from the bed wearing his discarded t-shirt I'd thrown on earlier. "I would have been there at 3 a.m. if I thought I could've dragged you and Maddox with me." He stepped closer, grasping my hip to pull me to him as Maddox lay cooing on the bed. "As it turned out, it was much better for me that we stayed here," he told me, taking my mouth in a quick but consuming kiss.

"For me, too," I agreed breathlessly.

"You wearin' my t-shirt?" he asked as I scooped Mad up and headed for the kitchen.

"Yeah," I shrugged.

"My dirty t-shirt," he amended, his eyes sweeping my frame.

"It smells good," I swallowed, trying to keep some semblance of sanity under his lust-inducing gaze.

"You smell good on me, too." He gave me a crooked smile and ran his fingers under his nose.

Holy hell.

The doorbell chimed loudly then, surprising us both.

"Go get some clothes on," Axel ordered, cocking his head toward the bedroom.

"Bossy," I mumbled, taking Mad with me to throw on some clothes as Axel stalked to the door.

When I re-entered the living room, I was surprised to see an older suit-clad man standing by the front door. He looked slightly nervous as he looked up at Axel's imposing figure as he stood guarding the man's entry with arms crossed.

"Miss Foster?" he presumed, peeking his head around Axel's large body and pushing his glasses further up his nose.

"Yes?" I answered, confused.

He sighed, looking relieved. "I'm so glad I tracked you down. I'm Frank Greenwood from JC Financials," he explained, though that didn't mean anything to me.

He must have seen the blank look on my face. "We manage your trust."

My brows knit in confusion as to what he'd be doing tracking me down. "Come in," I gestured, giving Axel a look to relax. He nodded once and moved further into the room gesturing that the man should have a seat.

"Coffee?" I offered.

"No, thank you," he shook his head as I took a seat nearby. Axel placed Mad in his Pack 'N Play with some toys and joined me.

"Miss Foster, your brother contacted us recently. He was concerned about statements you made that your parents had cut off your trust fund," he began as he opened up a briefcase and removed some documents. "We were very concerned and immediately investigated. What we uncovered is quite disturbing," he admitted with a sigh.

My mouth went dry as I waited for him to continue.

"It seems as though one or both of your parents have been intercepting your payments for the past year. Since we had no forwarding address for you and weren't aware you had left NY, the checks continued to go to them. It is also worth noting that a significant sum was left for your brother upon your grandfather's death that I'm just now able to provide to him."

"Did they try to steal that, too?" I asked quietly, bracing for his response.

"It would seem so," he admitted frankly.

"So they weren't able to actually cut off my fund then?" I asked, needing clarity.

"No," he shook his head. "Your grandfather left that money to you and was very explicit with the terms. This is why, despite the interception, your parents weren't able to successfully acquire any of yours or your brother's funds. I can't prove it but it seems they did in fact try to. I'm here to deliver the back pay from the past year and to confirm payments moving forward."

I looked over to Axel, needing him to center me in the whirlwind I'd suddenly been caught up in. He put his arm around me, pulling me into his warm body.

"Do her parents know you're here?" Axel's deep voice demanded, the rumble of his voice vibrating from his body.

"I'd imagine so," Mr. Greenwood nodded.

"They want control of those funds. That's what last night was about," Axel growled.

"I don't understand," I shook my head. "They're rich. Why do they want our money?"

"Maybe they're not so rich anymore," Axel surmised. "Can we press charges?" he asked Mr. Greenwood.

I stiffened, the reality of the situation slamming into my chest and causing my heart to fly.

"You can try," Mr. Greenwood nodded. "Though you might have difficulty making anything stick as the checks weren't cashed. Unless you can prove they made a concerted effort to acquire the funds they can claim they had no forwarding address and were simply holding on to the money."

"Shit," Axel growled.

"I'm sorry about this," Mr. Greenwood offered, seeming sincerely distressed. He handed me an envelope which I held in my lap.

"Is this the address future checks should be sent to?" he asked.

I looked to Axel. So much was yet to be worked out between us. Confirming an address felt like so much more. It meant not only that Maddox and I would be here, but that I trusted Axel in a way I couldn't even trust my own parents.

He held my gaze, his eyes glittering with emotion. "Yes." He confirmed Mr. Greenwood's question without breaking eye contact.

I looked back into his eyes knowing I was about to take a leap of faith.

"Yes, use this address." I nodded, looking toward the banker.

"Okay then," he stood, reaching out to shake both our hands. "I'm off to your brother's house now," he confirmed. "You two don't have the same last name?" he questioned as he straightened his jacket.

I shook my head. "We're half siblings. He was born with my mother's maiden name. I have my father's and what became my mother's married name," I explained, fighting back the urge to add that neither name was anything to write home about as it turned out.

He nodded in understanding.

"Thank you for coming out," I said, walking him to the door.

"Have a good day," he returned, clasping my hand briefly before turning and heading out to his car.

I looked down at the envelope in my hand. "I'm almost afraid to open it," I admitted quietly once we heard the banker's car rumble off down the road.

Ax pulled me close to his body, hugging me tightly. "You know we don't need it, right? I can take care of us. I will take care of us," he spoke, his voice low and commanding.

I looked up at him. "I know."

"All that time you struggled." He swallowed against the anger I saw rising to the surface. "You could have been taken care of. You wouldn't have had to work so damn hard."

I shook my head, stopping him from going down that road. "You know what? It's okay." I shrugged, shocking us both with my response. "Was it hard? Hell yes. But I proved a lot to myself. I took care of me and Mad after being sheltered and coddled my whole life. I'm glad to know I have that in me."

"You're so fucking strong, baby," he murmured

reverently, pulling me close again and rubbing his hands up and down my back.

In the end, we finished breakfast, got Mad dressed and only on our way out the door did I open the envelope.

I studied the sum, realizing not for the first time how money and privilege had stifled me throughout my life. It had constrained me with expectation and pedigree. I'd be damned if I let the same thing happen now – not when I was finally free.

I didn't want the life I knew in Hawthorne to change too much. It was shaping up beautifully as it was.

Chapter Eight

It was my first time at the club since I'd arrived back in town. We walked in with coffees in hand and I found myself feeling comforted by the smell of leather, engine grease and men. My eyes swept the common space noting that not much had changed. The pool table still sat in the corner near the bar. The pictures documenting the club's history still hung from the walls.

I smiled warmly as Cal, the club's president and Cole's father, wandered in from down the hall where they had a private meeting room and some other rooms whose purpose I didn't know.

Nor did I really want to.

"Sophie," he greeted with a grin that crinkled the edges of his beautiful blue eyes.

"Hi, Cal," I smiled, accepting his brief hug.

"We're glad to have you back," he noted sincerely, sweeping a large hand affectionately over Maddox's head. "No doubt who your daddy is," Cal chuckled, looking down at Mad.

Axel made a noise of approval in his throat in response.

Cal looked to Axel. "Hank and Wes are here, in the back. The rest of the guys are en route. He cocked his head toward the hall in silent direction that they head that way.

"Sure, be right there," Axel grunted before turning to me. "Sal's bringing Kat to hang with you. I've got to brief the guys. You gonna be okay?"

"Fine," I assured him.

Pride flickered on his face as he regarded me. "Good girl," he replied, stooping to kiss me briefly. I was surprised at the display of affection and it must have shown on my face. "Gonna take your mouth anytime, anywhere, babe," he assured me with a slow grin.

I nodded, liking the sound of that entirely too much.

It wasn't long before Sal and Kat swept into the room. Her belly seemed to be getting bigger by the day, protruding like a little beach ball on her thin frame.

"You all right, birdie?" Sal asked, eyeing her with concern.

"Fine," she sighed, sitting down on the couch with a huff.

"Hi, Soph," he added, grasping my shoulder briefly.

"Hey, Sal." I smiled as he swept a hand over Mad's head of hair. All the guys seemed to do this with him. It was such a tender gesture from such badass men.

"You get a visit this morning?" I asked with a cocked brow.

"Yep, fucking shocked the shit out of me." He shook his head, seeming stunned.

"I bet," I smiled softly.

"Now we just gotta figure out why the fuck another club would be trying to get at you," he growled. "That's way more important than some unexpected cash."

I nodded, watching him throw another concerned look to Kat before he stalked back to the offices.

Cole sauntered in not long after, followed by Mack, Tag and Xander.

"Where's Ryker?" I asked Kat, referring to Axel's younger brother.

"He's not patched in yet so he and Jeb don't get invited to these meetings," she informed me.

"Patched in?" I asked with a tilt of my head.

"Jeb and Ry are still prospects. There's a whole ceremony where they become officially part of the club. I think it might happen soon for Ry, not sure about Jeb."

"But he got stabbed trying to protect you!" I exclaimed, surprised he wouldn't be part of the club already. It was then I realized I hadn't seen Jeb around since being back.

She nodded. "I know, but I guess there's more to the story. I don't know the details," she shrugged.

I nodded, though I was still perplexed and went about setting up Mad's Pack 'N Play.

Kat kept me company while the guys met. We played with Maddox in the main room before taking him into the sunshine out back.

"You feeling okay?" I asked when I noticed how tired she looked.

"Yeah," she nodded. "The doctor just discovered my iron is really low which is why I've been so tired. I should be feeling better soon. Of course, Sal is acting like I've been diagnosed with something terminal." She rolled her eyes. "If he makes me another burger or tries to slip spinach into another smoothie, I'm going to throttle him."

I tried to smother my laughter but nodded sympathetically. "I know he can be overprotective but I'm glad you have someone to take care of you," I said.

Her eyes opened wide. "Oh, shit, Sophie, I didn't even

think about how you were alone. I must sound like an ungrateful bitch," she lamented.

"Not at all!" I rushed to assure her. "I'm just glad you and my brother have each other."

"Me, too." She reached over and squeezed my hand briefly.

"So what's all this about anyway?" she asked, cocking her head inside to where the guys were. "Sal didn't want to share much. I think he was too pissed to talk about it."

"Jill called me last night to say that some bikers broke into my old place. It seems as though they were Black Riders."

"Oh, shit, Axel must be ready to blow a gasket," she exclaimed when I was done.

"Just about," I agreed. "Now with what we learned this morning, Axel seems worried my father is somehow connected which…oh crap," I breathed, my eyes opening wide with realization.

"What?" she asked.

"All those things my father threatened me about, I never really questioned how he would have information on the club. He must be paying someone else from another club." I gasped, handing Mad to her and storming inside.

I paused in the hallway, afraid of interrupting their meeting. I knew there were all kinds of rules that I didn't yet understand. I wanted to respect that but I also needed to get to Axel.

I settled on texting him while pacing restlessly.

I heard the door open a second later and he stepped out, eyeing me warily. "Yeah, babe?"

"My father," I blurted, my hands on my hips. "He must have someone on the inside of another club! I didn't even think of it until now. That's how he had all the information about you before Mad was born. That must be who was looking for me now," I exclaimed in desperation.

"Uh, yeah, babe, I figured that was the case," he replied as though I were completely daft.

"You did?" I asked, shocked.

He had the gall the chuckle. "Baby, I appreciate that you thought you were bringing me late breaking news but it's pretty damn obvious. We're just trying to figure out who to throttle." He cocked his head toward the closed door.

"Oh," I replied lamely.

"Christ, you're cute." He chuckled again, pulling me closer and pressing his full lips to mine.

"I thought I was helping," I mumbled against his mouth.

"You can help me when Mad goes down for a nap," he grinned between kisses.

Heat pooled between my legs at the very thought. "I can do that," I whispered, my fingers tangling up into his thick hair and pulling slightly.

"Hey, love birds, save it," I heard Cal bark as Wes chortled in the background.

"I'll let you get back then," I blushed.

"Okay, darlin', see you in a few."

"Yeah," I agreed.

I grumbled my way back to Kat and Maddox. Apparently, my detective skills needed some serious help.

******

"Brake! Christ, babe," Axel half chuckled half groaned.

"I'm braking," I replied impatiently. "You're not very

good at this. For such a badass, you're kind of a pussy," I taunted before I had to bite back a laugh as he shot me a glare.

We'd dropped Mad off at Scarlet and Cole's for our date. Axel had insisted we start with a driving lesson, which is how we'd found ourselves in an abandoned parking lot in his F-150. His giant F-150.

"Couldn't I learn in Kat's old Corolla or something? This is ridiculous," I complained. "I feel like I'm driving a small country."

"You'll need an SUV for getting up the mountain in the winter, and anything after this will feel like a piece of cake."

I shot him a glare. "Is this how you're gonna teach Mad everything? The hardest way possible first?"

He shrugged. "Maybe."

"Great," I muttered.

"Let's practice parking," he suggested warily.

By the time we got to the restaurant, I was ready for a drink. He decided on a steakhouse just outside of town that Scar had mentioned more than once was amazing.

We sat at the bar while we waited for our table. I ordered a cosmopolitan while he sipped at a beer.

"I gotta head out of town later this week." He looked over at me with an appraising stare as though gauging my reaction.

"What? Why?" I asked with a mixture of disappointment at being away from him and straight anxiety about him being gone.

He hesitated and I narrowed my eyes. "Ax, remember what I said? I want to know what's going on."

He sighed and ran a hand over his beard. "A few of us

are riding out to take a meet with the Black Riders. Henry and a few of his guys are comin' too. We're trying to get to the bottom of this shit and we will." I'll be back as soon as I can. While I'm gone, you and Mad can stay with Sal."

It irritated me that he hadn't even asked me what I'd prefer.

"Actually, I'd rather not change Mad's surroundings again so soon. He's just starting to get used to your place and I like my sleep," I grumbled.

"I'd rather you were in town while I'm gone. The house is too isolated," he countered as he shook his head.

"Well, these are the types of conversations we should have before you make up your mind." I rolled my eyes.

"I'm not going to fuck around with your safety. You can be a pain in my ass all you want," he retorted.

"We still should talk about it first, geez!" I exclaimed. "I've taken orders all my life. I'm not about to do that again."

He gave me a look like he didn't know what the hell to do with me. He probably didn't. It occurred to me that while he was more experienced than I was in most ways, he'd never had a relationship like this before. We both had a learning curve to climb together.

"Listen," I began, my tone much softer. "You think I won't do what's best for Mad? All I'm asking is to be a part of the decision making process. I trust you to take care of us. But I need to be in charge of my own life. I need to have a say," I told him firmly.

He looked at me for a moment longer. "Fine," he agreed somewhat reluctantly. "Now, can we stop fucking fighting on our first date?" he demanded.

"It's our second date," I corrected him.

"Christ!" He threw up his hands in the air in exasperation.

I couldn't help it, I burst out laughing.

He pulled my stool closer to his, tilting me toward him so he could kiss me.

"Didn't know you had so much sass, but I like it," he admitted, his forehead pressed to mine.

"You bring it out in me," I shrugged with a smile.

Chapter Nine

The next evening, the club was packed with members and their families. Everyone was there, and at first, I was overwhelmed. Those I hadn't seen wanted to welcome me home and to meet Maddox.

It was a lot of attention all at once.

In particular, Axel's brother Ryker wanted to spend time with his nephew. You could certainly see the family resemblance between brothers. They were of similar height and build. Ry's hair was a bit lighter and his eyes were green rather than grey. In personality, they couldn't be more different. Where Axel was gruff and serious – most of the time anyway – Ry was a bit of a joker. He liked to lighten the mood whenever possible.

Maddox was passed around like a hot potato and I was moved by this positive change to his life. He'd gone from really only having me, to this large, boisterous group of extended family.

I sat with the girls, congratulating Ettie on her recent marriage to Mack as my eyes swept the space constantly ensuring I knew where Maddox was.

Like Scar and Kat, Ettie had her own battle scars from being kidnapped the previous year. I marveled at the strength and determination of the women around me. It gave me hope I'd get past my own situation and come out the other side better for it.

We'd been hanging out for a few hours when I watched warily as some of the club chicks perused the crowd as though seeking out any of the unattached men. The pickings were slimmer these days and I watched one woman, Bonnie I think was her name, zero in on Axel. My stomach dropped as I watched her approach with a sly smile. He didn't return it and their conversation was brief as she came flouncing back toward where I was sitting with her friend in tow.

"He didn't have a problem fucking me a few months ago," she huffed as she lit a cigarette.

"He'll come back around," her friend assured her as they moved out of earshot.

My stomach dropped and heart thumped painfully as I digested her words. Rationally, I knew I'd had no claim on him. But irrationally, the thought of him sleeping with her – especially while I'd been raising our son – well, it just plain hurt. There had been no one who measured up to him in my time away. No one. Obviously he hadn't had the same problem.

I swallowed hard, surprised at the strength of my response.

"Soph," Connie interrupted my mental tailspin with a squeeze of my thigh. Clearly, she'd observed the same things I had. "She isn't anything to him. We all know that," she assured me.

My cheeks flamed with embarrassment and I nodded, swallowing back tears I had no right to shed. I wanted to get out of there and wished fervently that I could drive.

Instead, I settled for moving inside away from the crowd. Kat had Maddox; he was in good hands and I could take a few minutes to collect myself.

I found a comfortable old leather chair that faced one of the windows and sat, trying to pull myself together. I heard the muted hum of everyone talking and laughing out back. It was rare for the inside of the club to be so still and I appreciated the quiet. I breathed in the stale smell of smoke and whiskey, finding the combination oddly comforting.

When Jeb approached, I smiled politely, though I was disappointed to have my time alone cut so short. This was the first time I'd seen him since I'd returned to town.

"Hi, Jeb," I greeted, surprised he was approaching me.

"Sorry, babe," he replied simply, his expression grim.

I had only a split second to let out a sharp scream as he placed something over my face. I struggled, my cries muffled as I breathed in the noxious fumes. It was only seconds before I was pulled under.

******

My head was absolutely pounding and my mouth felt like chalk when I started to come around an indeterminable amount of time later.

I heard deep male voices around me as I opened my burning eyes. What the hell had they knocked me out with? And why?

My blurry vision took a minute to focus and I saw that I was in a dimly lit motel room. The shades were drawn so it was impossible to tell what time of day it was. I was lying on the bed unrestrained and shifted slightly, my body feeling stiff and sore.

"She's awake," I heard an unfamiliar voice announce as my gaze shot in his direction.

He was an older man with jet-black hair and a goatee. His dark eyes fixed on me as I eyed the 'Black Riders' emblem on his jacket.

"Why? What's happening?" I asked Jeb hoarsely as he sat in a chair across the room.

He gave me a rueful grin. "Gotta get paid," he shrugged. "We figure your father will pay a high price for you."

This was insane.

I wanted desperately to ask about Maddox but was afraid to have my son even enter their minds. Jeb hadn't been around much. There was a remote chance he didn't even know I had a child.

I let out an ear-piercing scream then, hoping someone nearby would hear and call the cops.

Suddenly, a large hand was around my neck, squeezing briefly but enough to deliver a message. Jeb stared down at me his eyes wide. "You want me to gag you? I will, if you pull another stunt like that," he warned.

The fact that he hadn't already, made me feel like maybe there was some part of him that didn't want to do this. That gave me a small glimmer of hope in an otherwise bleak situation.

He let me go, tossing me back against the bed like a rag doll. I coughed, trying to catch my breath. "What about the Knights?" I asked, imploring him in a hoarse voice. Loyalty was so important to them and I had serious doubts he'd survive a betrayal like this.

He shrugged again then sneered. "After all I've done for those fucks, they still won't patch me in. Some shit about my dedication," he snorted, using quotation marks. "I was fucking stabbed for those shitheads and it still wasn't enough! So I found a club who'll patch me in." He shrugged as though this was perfectly logical.

I bit back the urge to retort that clearly their instincts had been right on about not patching him in.

"Enough fuckin' talkin'," the unfamiliar man barked. He was obviously the one in charge of this mess.

I looked between both men, racking my brain with how to buy more time. I knew Axel would be hunting for me. I just didn't know how the hell he'd find me. I also had no idea how long I'd actually been gone. My fuzzy brain tried to piece together a plan.

I looked to Jeb. "They're not going to let you into their club," I blurted, figuring distraction was my only real weapon. That, and clearly I had a much bigger brain than Jeb if he hadn't put this together.

Jeb turned to me with a mixture of anger and surprise. "What the fuck are you talking about?" he demanded.

"Come on, Jeb. Even I know enough about this stuff to know they wouldn't do that," I shook my head. "This guy here, I bet he's acting alone," I said, gesturing to the other man. "He gets the money and you're dead, I'd guess." I felt like my head was going to pound right off my neck as I nodded blearily. "His club isn't stupid enough to patch in a discarded member of the Knights." I swallowed, knowing I was taking a huge risk by pissing him off.

The smack to my face came so suddenly I didn't even see it coming. My head snapped to the right as the Black Rider's open hand connected with brutal force. "You want to survive this, I'd shut that pretty little mouth," he growled.

My ears were ringing and I tasted blood. I was taking a chance in thinking that if they wanted their money, they'd know to keep me in one piece. But there was only so far I wanted to push that theory.

My hand moved to my throbbing face as I watched them both in silence.

"Dude, is she right?" Jeb demanded, his tone betraying the worry I'd planted.

"No," the man barked. "Now shut the fuck up, both of you."

"I want to know what the fuck she knows that I don't," Jeb continued stubbornly, his eyes wide with panic.

"She doesn't know shit," the man retorted, losing patience. "She's graspin', trying to stress you out. Chill the fuck out."

I looked to Jeb, watching the slow wheels of his brain begin to crank.

"Jeb, if this guy doesn't kill you – the Knights will if you go through with this," I spoke up, despite knowing the consequences. I had to try to talk him out of this. Jeb wasn't nearly as smart as the other guy – that much was clear. If I could get him scared enough, maybe I could swing things in my favor. "Let me go," I demanded passionately as the other man stormed across the room and pulled me to my feet.

My heart pounded in my chest as fear raced through my bloodstream.

"You're either brave or really fucking stupid." His eyes were cold and calculating as he pulled me up so that our faces were inches apart. "You're beautiful, too." His eyes raked over my frame, remaining on my chest far too long for my comfort.

"You wanna give me a taste?" he leered, his head cocked to the side. His fingers moved to my top, unbuttoning the first three buttons.

"You touch me again you won't see a dime," I replied, my tone far braver than I felt. I was dangerously close to completely losing any semblance of bravery.

If my father had in fact orchestrated this, I had to at least cling to the hope he'd request I be unharmed. I wanted to curl up in a ball and scream for Axel, but that wouldn't get me back to him or Maddox any faster.

He shrugged and licked his lips. "You're probably right. Might be worth it, though."

"Come on, Aron, stop fucking around," Jeb cut in, using the man's name for the first time.

Aron turned his dark eyes to Jeb, shoving me back onto the bed as he stalked in his direction. He punched Jeb hard in the face and I reeled back in shock as the two men began to fight in earnest. "You do not call the shots, boy. You got that?" Aron grunted as he gained the upper hand.

I used their distraction to my advantage. I couldn't make it to the front door since they were right in front of it, but I sprinted to the bathroom, locking it behind me. My whole body shook with panic as they immediately began banging on the door. I vaulted up to the tiny window, trying with all my might to shove it open. It groaned and rattled in protest on its hinges before I opened it with enough force to shatter the glass.

If I was injured, the adrenalin pumping through my veins made it so I didn't feel anything but the fierce need to escape. I was able to hoist myself through the small space screaming the entire time, praying someone would call the police. I landed in the concrete hallway and started to run.

I didn't know where the hell I was going, but putting the motel behind me was all I cared about.

I staggered into the parking lot looking frantically right and then left, hoping it'd be clear which way to turn.

I heard the rumble of bikes before I saw them. For a moment, I was terrified it was Black Riders until I saw the familiar bikes and SUVs come careening into view.

It was the most beautiful sight I'd ever seen.

I fell to my knees, the superhuman strength I'd been exhibiting leaving me in a rush now that I knew I was rescued.

"Fuck!" I heard Axel's voice roar as car doors slammed and bike engines cut to silence all around me. He was soon sliding to his knees in front of me, his large hands cupping my jaw, his gentleness juxtaposing his thunderous expression. "Baby," his voice caught as he assessed the damage.

From his expression, I was guessing I didn't look too good. I was aware of activity around me. Many of the guys went running toward the motel shouting commands to each other.

I was finally able to ask the one question that had been burning in my brain since this had all started. "Maddox?" I rasped out.

"He's fine, baby," Axel was quick to reassure me.

"Shit, Sophie." Sal's tense voice came to me from above. I looked up to find my brother staring down at me with pain and anger glittering in his dark eyes.

"Where are you hurt?" Axel demanded as his eyes roamed my face.

"I-I think just my face and where the glass from the window cut me," I answered, confused and overwhelmed.

"I'm kind of out of it." I looked down at my bloody arms. It was as though I was having an out of body experience, like this wasn't really happening to me.

"What do you mean?" he asked with quiet intensity.

"He knocked me out with something and then I got smacked around pretty good," I murmured, my hands moving to my throbbing temples. Had I been thinking clearly I would have thought more about what this news would do to him.

His expression froze, his eyes blazing with fury.

He stood, lifting me in his arms bridal style as Sal strode alongside us. Suddenly, gunshots pierced the evening air and my whole body shook with renewed fear. If anyone I cared about got hurt over this, I'd never forgive myself.

Axel lifted me into the passenger side of an SUV and quickly draped his jacket over me. I hadn't realized that my clothes were torn to shreds. He turned to me with an expression so dark I barely recognized him. "Your brother is going to take you to get checked out. I'll be there as soon as I can." His gaze locked on the motel beyond.

"What? You can't leave me!" I exclaimed in a panic, clutching his shirt in my hands.

Sal put a hand on his shoulder, the only display of friendship I'd seen between them since I'd been back. Despite the initial truce they'd come to in Dallas, things had still been tense between them.

"I know what you're feeling, brother. Believe me, I do," Sal grit out. "But she needs you right now more than you need retribution. Got me?"

Axel's massive chest heaved as he blew out a ragged breath, trying to pull himself together. He looked like a caged beast as he met my brother's gaze. "Their blood.

It's mine," he growled, pointing a finger toward the motel. "You promise me that."

"I swear it," Sal agreed, grasping the back of Axel's neck as the two men touched foreheads briefly. "Take care of my sister. She needs you." I knew this was huge for them both.

Axel blew out a breath trying to rein in his anger. "Yeah, man," he agreed just as the guys returned hauling Aron and Jeb forcefully out to the parking lot.

Axel strode over to where Cole restrained Jeb, his long legs eating the space as he moved to take Jeb's neck in his firm grip. I couldn't hear what he said but Jeb's face paled more than it already was.

Then he was returning to me, his expression softening as he pulled my seatbelt on before moving around to the driver's side.

"No hospital," I mumbled, fighting against my drooping eyelids. The adrenaline had fully crashed and I was feeling it.

"Babe," he protested.

"No. Hospital," I reiterated. "If you need to, call Jill, she'll help," I grit out, trying hard to hide my pain.

"Jill's in Dallas," he argued.

"She'll help," I replied stubbornly.

He sighed but fell quiet. I took that as a good sign I'd get my way and allowed my eyelids to win the battle they'd been waging since the SUV started up.

Chapter Ten

I woke up when the motor cut. I looked out the window with bleary eyes, relieved to see we were at Axel's.

"Is Mad here?" I asked as Axel came to my side and lifted me out, moving to carry me inside.

"No, babe, he's with Scarlet. Cal's there, too. Someone will either bring him home or we'll get him in the morning, okay?"

I bit my lip against the disappointment. "Okay," I answered. After a night like this, I wanted nothing else but to hold my boy.

"Tonight, I need to take care of you," he added quietly, stepping into the quiet house.

"What time is it?" I thought to ask, wondering how long I'd been in that godforsaken motel room.

"Just after two," he replied. "Seven hours," he added grimly, recognizing the direction of my thoughts.

He moved us to the bathroom, sitting me carefully on the counter. I couldn't get a handle on his expression as he looked me over. He looked haunted.

"What is it?" I asked quietly.

He swallowed audibly. "I'm gonna have to take the glass out," he explained in a deep, troubled voice. "Your perfect fucking skin." He looked dangerously close to losing it again like he had back at the motel.

"Hey," I put a hand on his arm, the muscle flexing with tension under my touch. "I'm tougher than I look," I assured him with a small smile.

He looked me in the eye, his eyes a lighter grey than I'd ever seen as tension knitted his brow. "I can take on five men," he rasped as I wondered where he was going with this. "I've been stabbed. Shot once," he added, his hand moving to the puckered scar I noticed before on his shoulder. "I grew up with a violent father whose acts against me, my brother and my mother were unconscionable."

My eyes pooled with tears as he shared this piece of himself with me. I knew his childhood hadn't been a happy one. I knew he had a darkness in him that when freed could envelop any light. I'd always wanted to know where it came from. He'd never spoke about his father and I wanted desperately to understand what he'd been through. But this wasn't the time.

He moved a hand through my hair as his eyes locked on the movement of his fingers gliding through my chestnut strands. "I'd sooner go through all that again. Hell, I'd do it all at the same fucking time if it meant I didn't have to cause you more pain right now." He swallowed.

I took his huge hand in mine, squeezing tightly, giving him what little comfort I could. "I know it might be selfish," I explained quietly. "But I need it to be you. Everything's all screwed up and your hands are the only ones I want on me." His grey eyes snapped to mine. "It won't hurt as bad if it's you," I added.

He nodded, straightening to his full height. "All right, baby," he rasped.

It took thirty horrible minutes to pull out every shard of glass from my skin. The hardest part was hiding my reaction. I knew it would make it so much harder on him if I showed my pain. So I bit it back with everything I had, even as the tweezers dove in deep.

"Goddammit, Sophie, I know this has to be fucking agony!" he swore when we were nearly done. "Don't hide your pain from me! Give it to me so I can take it from you."

I nodded, letting the tears fall freely as I sucked in a ragged breath. It did feel better not to have to hide it. "How did you find me?" I asked, wincing as he pulled another shard out.

"I can't talk about tonight right now, baby. I'll lose my shit. Later, okay? I'll tell you everything I know," he assured me.

I appreciated that he knew I'd want to know the details. "Okay," I agreed.

"Jill wants to come out," he told me, sensing I needed to talk about something, anything.

"Really?" I asked. "When did you talk to her?"

"On the drive home, you were out," he murmured. "She's worried about you but I also got the sense things may not be so great in Dallas."

I felt my brow crease. "But Tim just got home."

He shrugged. "I don't know the details but she seemed eager to come out," he continued, his brow furrowed in concentration as he pulled the last shard out of my upper arm. "Okay, baby, let's get you in the shower," he sighed, seeming as relieved as I was that it was over.

I nodded as he helped me off the counter, undressing me carefully. He undressed as well and guided us under the warm water, pulling me against his broad chest, kissing the top of my head.

He cupped the sides of my head, tilting my face upwards, his fingers running over my split lip. "I swore to you I'd protect you," his deep voice rasped. "I never thought one of my own brothers would pull this shit."

"You couldn't have known." I shook my head, wanting to assuage his guilt. "I shouldn't have wandered away by myself," I added quietly. "I just couldn't deal with that chick talking about you." I took a deep shaky breath, my eyes sliding to the side.

His brows knit in confusion. "What?"

"I watched her come up to you at the club," I began.

"Eyes," he commanded gruffly, forcing me as he so often did to look at him when I shared something especially difficult.

"She walked away from you talking with her friend about how she'd slept with you. I know I have no right but it was hard to hear," I admitted quietly. "So I went inside for a few minutes to have some time to pull it together."

He moved his fingers through my hair, tugging gently in a way that made me want to purr. "I've never been a one-woman man," he began, and I tensed, not liking the sound of that. "Until you." He swallowed thickly, his hands running over my shoulders and gently down my cut arms. "That won't be the last time you hear shit like that." He shook his head. "But I want it to be the only time it bothers you. You're all I see," he said gruffly, the emotion in his voice making my heart flutter. "I want you to understand that you're the only woman who I've wanted under my roof. You're the only woman who's ever been under my skin. Had I known you were out there raisin' my kid alone." He shook his head, his expression pained. "I didn't think you were ever coming back, Soph." His voice was like gravel as he forced the words out.

"I know," I cut him off, not able to bear him continuing.

"Tonight when I couldn't find you – when I didn't know what happened to you, I've never felt anything like that." He blew out a breath. "I would have torn up this goddamn Earth to find you, Sophie."

"I know," I whispered again as he pulled me back against his chest to hold me.

"Let's get you to bed," he coaxed as he reached around me to turn the water off, helping me to step out of the shower.

I bobbed my head in agreement. It was about all I could manage.

I lay on my side, facing him, my hands tucked under my cheek. He clicked off the light and slid into bed, lying on his back, his hand placed over his muscular stomach.

"What are you thinking?" I asked, the darkness giving me confidence I wouldn't have had otherwise.

Those eyes of his always seemed to slay me.

"I'm thinking that you're really fucking brave," his deep voice returned.

"Me?"

"Yes, you."

I heard his head rustle on the pillow as he turned toward me. "You grew up totally sheltered, almost completely controlled by your parents. Yet you have a fight in you that would have long ago died out in a lot of other people. You didn't accept what was being forced on you. You did what you had to do to protect our son to try to make a life for yourself from nothing. As much as I wish you would have trusted me, as much as I wish I could have been a part of every minute, I'm still so fucking proud. Even tonight, you didn't accept that shit. You fought to the bitter end. If that's not the definition of bravery then, darlin', I don't know what is."

That he saw me like that was empowering. It was also beautiful. "Thanks," I managed, quietly.

"For what?" he asked.

"For seeing me like that, as I really am or how I'd like to be, anyway. And for what sounds like you forgiving me." I choked out the last part as warm tears slid to the pillow. "But I still don't get why after all the women…why I'm the one…" I trailed off.

His calloused hands stroked my tears away. "It's tough to put words to. I've never felt it before. But, you're my girl. You're sweetness and light, and you look at me with such richness that I feel fucking full. I felt that way the moment I laid eyes on you when you were sitting on that stoop in New York."

"Those are some pretty good words."

His hand reached out to stroke my hair back from my face. "We're not as different as you may think. I know what it's like to feel powerless – to want something more. It's part of why I was so drawn to you. I understand that side of you – that ferocity to fight despite your outward fear. And, shit, you fit in with my crew better than most other women would. You don't take any shit and yet your heart is so warm. They all adore you. You entered our world like you'd always been there – and I'm gonna make sure that's where you stay," he told me, his finger gliding down my cheek.

I was floored by this side of Axel. This tough, badass biker with words so eloquent they should be written and remembered.

"There's no place else I'd rather be," I assured him. We lay in silence for a few moments before I spoke again. "How'd you find me?"

He scrubbed a hand over his face and let out a low sound of frustration. I knew he didn't want to talk about it, not yet, but I had to know what information there was to be had.

"I want to know," I pressed.

Finally, he nodded. "Jeb's been actin' shady for a while now," he began as I listened intently. "Ever since he got injured protecting Kat, he seemed to think he was immediately entitled to be patched in. When that wasn't the case, he started to distance himself from the club. He seemed bitter. Put us on edge, especially your brother. He knew from all that shit with Allen Parker that prospects can get some sense of entitlement." He snorted.

I didn't know much about Allen Parker other than he'd had a vendetta against the Knights, which Kat had ended up being the center of.

"Fuckin' assholes think they can put in a few months of hard work and be part of a club." He shook his head. "Anyway, I didn't know it until tonight but Sal had started tracking Jeb. When you disappeared...fuck!" He shook his head. "It took a while for us to realize what happened. Then we didn't know how long you'd been gone." I rolled closer to him, wanting the contact while he shared the rest. "I knew you wouldn't just up and leave Maddox." His deep voice rumbled under my cheek as I pressed close. "It was Mack who suggested Jeb. At first, we thought he was fucking crazy." Axel made a scoffing sound low in his throat. "I mean, we knew he was off the rails a little but taking you would be signing his own death warrant. Then the pieces started coming together with the shit with the Black Riders. We figured Jeb was holdin' a grudge for not getting patched in."

"You were right," I confirmed, burrowing closer still as his strong arm pulled me tightly against his warmth.

"Sal gunned it to his place to activate the tracking shit he'd put in Jeb's cell. Bastard must've ditched it or left it somewhere. That's why it took us so long. But we got close enough to figure it out. There isn't much out that way," he explained, referring to the motel.

I shuddered, thinking of what would have happened if they hadn't have shown up.

"Hey, don't think about it. I can't," he admitted, his voice thick with emotion.

I placed my hand on his abs, the muscles clenching underneath my touch and I kissed his chest, moving upward to his neck. His breathing immediately grew harsh and I was encouraged even more to continue. His face turned toward me and I touched his lips with mine.

Reaching over, his hand clasped the back of my neck as he pulled me in for a passionate kiss. He moved my body over his so I was straddling him. I sucked in a ragged breath, feeling his hardness against my skin.

"Baby, you're all cut up," he protested, his breathing ragged.

"I need this. Don't stop," I pleaded, adding a ragged, "Please."

His hand reached up under the shirt I wore to trace the bare skin of my back before moving to the front and finding my breasts. He tweaked both nipples firmly, growling into my mouth with a sound of such pleasure that my core nearly liquefied.

He felt like steel where he was pressed to my center as he sat up, sweeping my shirt over my head and his lips replaced his fingers.

I sucked in a breath and moaned loudly, the noise escaping my lips still foreign in my ears.

"Christ, you are so fucking gorgeous." His lips moved over my breast, taking a nipple and sucking voraciously.

He rolled us so he was on top, pressing between my legs as he took my mouth in a passionate onslaught. His hand stroked over my belly, sliding lower until he reached my panty line.

"So wet for me," he breathed reverently as his fingers dipped underneath the fabric.

"Yes."

He feasted on my body with his mouth, his teeth finding purchase in my pliant skin as he went. When he reached my core and feasted, I was moved quickly beyond sanity.

He brought me to the breaking point before rising above me and gliding inside.

The feeling of him inside me with nothing separating us was enough to make me momentarily lose my mind. "I'm not on anything," I managed, despite the excitement that threatened to eclipse rational thought.

He paused, looking down at me. "I've never not used anything, baby. I'm clean. I'll pull out but you feel so damn good," he rasped.

I looked up at him, my fingers trailing the whiskers along his jaw. "There's only ever been you."

His eyes blazed with that knowledge. "I want you on top," he growled, biting gently at my neck before shifting our bodies so that he lay beneath me.

Despite the desperation I felt to have him, I was out of sorts and unsure in this position. My inexperience and insecurity was front and center in a way I wasn't ready for.

I shook my head. "No I…" I drifted off, trying to move away from him.

His hands griped my forearms like a vise as his eyes shone with intensity up into mine. "You look so fucking sexy like this, baby," he growled, halting my escape.

"I don't know what I'm doing," I admitted with a whisper, though I was motivated to figure it out by his appreciative gaze.

He took my hips in his hands, guiding my movements. "Just do what feels good," he coaxed with a rasp.

I shifted my hips forward my palms splayed across his chest.

"Fuck," he bit out.

"You're so deep like this," I gasped as I leaned forward, finding the angle that worked best.

His hands lifted, his fingers tweaking my nipples as I took him. He let me experiment for a while until we were both at the breaking point. I felt him shift then, his heels firmly planted in the mattress as he took me from the bottom. He powered up, causing me to cry out.

He let out a groan, pulling me bodily beneath him in a fluid movement.

I shattered seconds later with him soon pulling out of me with a low groan as he let loose across my belly.

"That was fun," I laughed into his neck as I fought to catch my breath.

"You have no idea how much fun we're going to have," he responded with a devilish grin.

We cleaned up together in the bathroom before turning

in.

"Night, baby."

"Night," I murmured, burrowing closer to his skin.

Chapter Eleven

"Soph," Ax's voice cut through my deep sleep.

"Hmm. Mmm?"

"I gotta go. Mad's in his crib. Ry's on the couch. Get some sleep," he murmured, his lips brushing my neck.

"Mad?" I rasped, feeling more awake.

"Ry brought him back. Everything's good," he assured me.

"Where're you going?" I mumbled.

"I've gotta take care of some loose ends," he answered vaguely.

It wasn't until hours later when I was fully awake that I realized what that really meant.

I fell back asleep after he left, for how long I wasn't sure, before Maddox was cooing from the other room. I stretched out briefly, Axel's side of the bed cool to the touch. My entire body felt sore but I didn't feel as bad as I would have expected. I opened the office door, finding Mad sitting up in his crib with a big grin on his face.

There was never a finer sight.

When I moseyed out to the kitchen with Maddox on my hip, I stopped short at Ryker snoring on the couch. I'd nearly forgotten he'd be there.

I was intending to be as quiet as possible but almost immediately, Maddox let out a loud shriek of glee at seeing his bottle. Ryker was so shocked, he toppled off the couch.

"Sorry," I apologized through laughter as he looked around, as though he had to remember where he was.

"Jesus, that kid is loud," he groused, running a hand through his hair and rising to his feet.

"Babies tend to be loud," I agreed. "I'll make coffee."

"Thank God," he muttered.

"Heard from your brother?" I asked, my tone deliberately casual.

"Unless he spoke to me in my sleep, then no," he retorted.

"You're not a morning person then," I surmised dryly.

"She's quick on her feet," he muttered sarcastically. "How're you feeling?" His tone was softer as his eyes swept over the visible cuts on my arms and my swollen lip.

"I'm okay," I assured him as I rummaged around trying to make coffee.

"I can take him," Ryker offered, cocking a brow at Mad.

"Really? Okay," I shrugged, passing off my son. He seemed perfectly content in his uncle's arms.

"You're really okay? That was a fucked-up night," he pressed, dodging Mad's attempts to grab his lip.

"I've been better," I admitted. "But I know your brother's gonna take care of it." I realized how much that soothed me as I said it. I had a man at my back who would willingly take on an army for me.

"Yeah, he is," Ryker agreed. "Never thought I'd see the guy be such a goner," he commented, but the look on his face gave me pause.

"Is that a bad thing?" I cajoled with a grin.

He shrugged. "Just can't see one chick doin' it for me." His eyes shifted to the side and I was sure I detected something there.

A lie?

I cocked my head to the side.

"Except for one," he allowed so quietly I barely heard him. "Don't ask."

I studied him for a moment. "Okay," I agreed, biting back my intense curiosity.

"Whether it's this mystery girl or someone else, when you meet your lady I'm gonna give you so much shit," I promised, lightening the mood.

"Did you just cuss, sis?" he teased. "And fine, if I fall off the cliff like my brother has, you can give me all the shit you want."

"I'm counting on that," I nodded with a grin.

******

Axel didn't get home until close to lunchtime. He walked in with a dark expression, scanning the room as though searching for a threat. My eyes shot to his bloody knuckles and back to his eyes trying to find the man in there I knew.

The man I loved.

"Hey, honey," I greeted softly, moving to greet him by the door where he still stood, his posture stiff and unwelcoming. I was in unfamiliar territory with him and I hoped like hell I could pull him out of this mood. "You hungry?"

He shook his head. "Where's Maddox?" he asked in a hoarse murmur.

"Napping. Your brother's downstairs on the computer. What is it?" I asked quietly, placing a tentative hand to his chest.

He pulled me to his chest, lifting me up so that I instinctively wrapped my arms around his neck and my legs around his waist. "He's gonna be on the computer a little while longer," he stated gruffly, carrying me to his – our –room.

My entire body hummed as he carried me briskly back to his room. "Ry! Stay downstairs," he barked.

"Yeah, man," I heard Ry reply through the walls as Axel strode into our room and all but kicked the door shut.

He really needed to learn to be quieter with a baby in the house but now definitely wasn't the time to remind him.

"What?" I tried to ask but was cut off by his lips covering mine with a kiss that made me forget all thought. His hands were all over my body, tearing at my clothes as his chest heaved.

"You good?" he demanded, his tongue finding the spot behind my ear that made me crazy. Who would have thought?

"Yeah," I replied breathlessly. I wanted to be the balm that soothed him. I knew he needed this, needed me and I was more than willing.

I pulled his shirt up over my head, my hands roaming the chiseled muscle and warm skin I found underneath. Then I shocked myself by dropping to my knees, looking up at him as I unbuckled his belt and pulled his jeans down his legs.

"Christ," he swore, watching me with stormy eyes as I licked him from root to tip. I'd never done this before but I wanted nothing more in the world than to please him this way.

Moisture pooled between my legs as I relished the taste and feel of him. He was all velvety smoothness and coiled tension.

Suddenly, I was pulled up and practically thrown on the bed. "You keep doing that I'm gonna lose it, and I need to be inside you," he explained as he sheathed himself with a condom. His large body came up over mine, his muscles tense and rippling as he moved. Then he was inside me with one fluid thrust. I bit back the cry threatening to break free as he moved with an urgency I'd never seen in him before. Every time with him had been a claiming of sorts but this was utterly primal. His body completely owned mine as his lips found every surface they could reach, his teeth raking across my flesh.

The temperature of my skin blazed with my impending orgasm and I was nearly afraid of what it would do to me.

"Let it go, baby," he commanded, his hand reaching between our bodies, his fingers dancing over my clit. That was it. I reached desperately for a pillow, clamping it over my face as I let out an uncontrollable cry. He pulled it away almost immediately, looking down on me as his movements became more erratic before he groaned low and deep, collapsing on top of me.

I held him to me, wrapping my legs and arms around his big body as we both fought to catch our breath.

"Are you okay? Shit, I didn't mean to be so rough," he admonished himself as his fingers swept over my lip and down my arm.

"I'm fine," I assured him, meaning it. "Are you okay?"

He pulled back from me, eyeing me warily. "Yeah, I

just…needed you, I guess," he admitted, his face twisting in a grimace.

"Is that bad?" I asked softly.

He shrugged. "Guess not, just new."

"For me, too," I nodded with a smile. "What happened?" I pressed, my hands sweeping through his thick hair.

"It doesn't seem like your father ordered the kidnapping," he shared, shaking his head. "It seems like Aron thought he'd discovered an easy payday by coming up with a scheme to deliver you to him. Pretty damn sure he planned to off Jeb once he got paid. Fucking idiots," he grumbled.

Some of the tension I hadn't even realized I'd been holding slowly released from my body.

His expression softened as he looked down at me. "You're relieved," he assessed.

I bit my lip. "Well, yeah," I shrugged. "I mean, I know my father has less than stellar morals but even I didn't think he'd sink so low as to kidnap me!" I exclaimed.

"I understand, darlin'. Believe me, I know something about holding out hope that you don't come from total shit," he muttered. "But this doesn't mean he's not a threat, darlin'."

"I know," I agreed quietly.

"He has some connection with the Black Riders. We still have to figure out if there's another leak or if those fucks were all there was," he told me, rising up off me and offering his hand. He pulled me up into his arms, kissing me soundly. "But the message has been delivered that you're mine and that anyone who hurts you will fucking pay," he told me, his countenance suddenly fierce.

I didn't doubt that was true.

"Uh, guys?" I heard a tentative voice call from the hallway. "I've got a guy out here with a full diaper and an uncle who doesn't know, or want to know how, to take care of it," Ryker hollered.

I rolled my eyes at Axel and he chuckled. "Coming!" I called.

Chapter Twelve

"Goddammit, Sophie, block! Remember?" Axel demanded, frustrated as I struggled to focus. It would really help if he wasn't only wearing black shorts and a grimace. I was totally distracted by his body and his proximity. Every time he came near, I just thought of ways to bring him closer rather than ways to push him back.

"Yeah," I nodded, panting slightly with exertion.

We'd been at it awhile, practicing at the gym as we'd done for the past two weeks. They had a boxing room set apart from the gym itself, which allowed us privacy to train.

Ever since my kidnapping, I'd struggled with nightmares, with a fear of being helpless. So Axel was teaching me how to fight back. For the most part, it was helping – so long as I tried not to let my beautiful man distract me.

I'd long since ditched my tank top, and my pink sports bra was soaked through. If he was going to wear so little, why should I suffer from heat exhaustion?

"We gonna actually get through the floor work today?" he asked with a raised brow and a look of mischief in his light eyes.

We ended up in the equipment room closet more times than not.

"I'll try to control myself," I muttered sarcastically. Though in reality, I wasn't so sure about that.

His gaze swept my frame and he licked his lips. He was deliberately baiting me.

I screwed my face up in a grimace and huffed my frustration.

He threw his head back and laughed, hard. Even though it was at my expense, I still appreciated the sound – so rich and sincere. He laughed with his whole body, his hands clutching at his abs, his muscles flexing with the movement.

"I don't see what's so funny," I mumbled.

"You are!" He grinned, winking. "I swear I've laughed more with you than I ever have in my life and you aren't even tryin'," he proclaimed, more to himself than to me.

"Glad to be of service," I grumbled.

Then he was in my space in a way I was unprepared for, his glistening chest inches from my face. His knuckle ducked under my chin, tipping my face up to meet his gorgeous countenance. "Soph," he started quietly, his tone suddenly far more serious. "As much as I want inside you, I want you to be able to protect yourself more. It's time to get into it. Are you ready?" he asked quietly, peering into my face in a way that always disarmed me.

I swallowed hard. "Yeah, let's just do it," I sighed.

"You sure?" His face betrayed so much concern for me; it nearly broke my heart. With that realization, I needed to do this as much for him as for me. I wanted to make him proud. To show both of us that I could do this.

"Yeah," I agreed, determined to push past my nerves.

"We've walked through this. You know the drill," he explained. "I'm going to pin you and you're going to use your knees, fingernails and elbows," he reminded me of what we'd walked through many times before.

"Yeah." I nodded as I swallowed hard.

Then he was on me; he didn't even give me a second. He took me to the ground with brute force so overwhelming I froze up entirely.

"Soph," his voice rumbled in my ear as he reminded me of where I was and who I was with.

All I could hear was the clanging of my heartbeat. All I could feel was the crushing weight of his body.

He leaned down into me, and with a subtle shift of his body, he changed the tenor of the situation. There was nothing sexual or fearsome in his proximity, only comfort. "You don't at least try and we're eating Mariachi's for dinner," he threatened.

His teasing tone and mention of my least favorite restaurant in Hawthorne somehow broke through my fear-induced haze.

I managed a look at him, up into his sincere eyes that peered down, so close to mine.

"Not Mariachi's," I grimaced, so grateful to him in that moment for making light of the situation rather than delving into it. In so many ways, he understood me better than anyone.

"Then show me what you're made of," he challenged, his eyes gleaming with encouragement.

And I did.

I brushed everything aside and I gave him a mock thrust to the groin, shove to the throat and rolled us so I straddled him.

He looked up at me with pride lighting his normally somber face. "Good job, baby," he grinned.

I sagged into him, not caring we were both covered in sweat. I laid my body down on top of his, my face buried in his neck, breathing in his richly masculine scent. "Thanks," I murmured.

His arms came up around me, caging me in the most delicious way, rewarding me for challenging myself by offering me what I'd needed all along…comfort in its purest form. Our bodies pressed together like this in any other situation would have set every synapse I had on fire, but hot and sweaty on the gym floor as we were, it just offered calm and safety.

"You did good," he whispered in my ear.

"Thanks," I sighed.

We laid there for an indeterminable amount of time against the blue mat in the nearly empty gym, the sound of treadmills droning in the distance the only sound.

"Let's go get our little man," he suggested, sitting up with me still plastered to his front. Mad had been with his Auntie Kat for the morning. We had so much help with Maddox; it was amazing.

I reluctantly pried myself away, moving to stand and straighten myself. "Yeah," I agreed.

"Here," he said, handing me my long since discarded shirt.

"I'm still so hot. I'm just headed to the showers anyway." I wrinkled my brow.

His eyes narrowed as he stepped closer. "You're not walking through the gym like that. Put it on," he ordered.

"Fine," I huffed, snatching it out of his hand and

pulling it over my head. "Put this on then," I challenged with a raised brow, handing him his own shirt. If I had to cover up, then he did too.

He rolled his eyes but took the shirt from me, yanking it down over his head. "Happy?"

"Thrilled." I grinned as his phone rang.

"Hey, Ry," he greeted his brother, his eyes trained on me. I watched his brow crease before his expression grew hard. "No, I've got Soph, but I'll take care of it." He paused for a minute, his stance tense. "No, Ry, I got it. Call you later."

"What is it?" I asked quietly after he ended the call.

"Some shit with my ma," he grumbled. "I'll drop you at Sal's and head out for a while," he told me.

I studied him for a moment, taking in his guarded expression and stiff posture. I knew his childhood had been dysfunctional at best. Aside from that, I didn't know much. He was always protecting everyone else, even his brother. I wanted him to know he could rely on me to do the same for him.

"I want to come," I replied firmly.

"What? No." He shook his head as he stalked past me.

"Kat will watch Mad a while longer," I grabbed his arm and pulled him around to face me. "Let me come, please, babe," I practically pleaded.

His hand went to the back of his neck in a gesture I recognized as stress. "Why?" he asked, seeming positively bewildered by my request. "It'll be a total shit situation. I can pretty much guarantee that."

"That's why I want to come," I explained gently.

We regarded each other for a moment in a battle of wills before he sighed. "Fine, but don't say I didn't warn you."

"Deal," I agreed, trying not to tap dance in satisfaction that I'd won this round. We'd both be better for it; I could feel it.

We rode for a good thirty minutes, passing the club on our way out of town. I loved being on the back of his bike, the motor humming beneath me and the wind whipping through my hair.

We entered a part of Nevada I'd yet to see. The area grew more remote as we sped along the highway, pulling off along a long dirt road.

The dilapidated houses I caught glimpses of fought with the desert for survival against the intensity of the sun. The bike slowed as we pulled onto a dusty drive that led to a small single-story house. It must have been yellow at one time but the paint had long since faded with the power of the sun. The front yard was littered with weeds, a bit of trash and a lone garden gnome.

It was the saddest goddamned gnome I'd ever seen, despite his tenacious smile.

"Wait here," Axel growled, clearly not pleased I'd practically demanded I come along.

He swung off the bike, stalking toward the tiny house, practically swinging the front door from its hinges as he pushed his way inside.

I got off the bike, removed my helmet and eyed the house with morbid curiosity.

Was this where he'd grown up? The thought made my heart clench.

I sat, leaning against the bike for what felt like forever with the sun beating down on me.

I heard some sort of commotion inside that sounded

like breaking glass and immediately grew concerned. I hadn't come along to be kept at arm's length and decided I'd given him enough time before I joined him.

All I could hear from the front stoop was a low grunt of effort and what sounded like a quiet murmur. It didn't sound like any sort of struggle or imminent danger so I pulled the screen door open, the creaking sound echoing through the vastness of the desert at my back.

"Ax?" I called softly.

"Back to the bike, Soph," he grunted with impatience, sounding like he was trying to carry something heavy.

"Let me help," I said, bravely entering the house. Immediately, the stench of vomit filled my nose and I recoiled. It was both fresh and stale making for a stomach churning combination. I stood in a tiny living room that was surprisingly neat with two couches and a small coffee table filling the space. The pictures on the mantel caught my eye, a young clean-shaven Axel smiling in what looked like a high school photograph. Beside it, an even younger looking Ryker.

I heard another noise from down the hall and rushed to help. When I came to the first bedroom on the right, I stopped short.

Axel was trying to haul an older, very drunk woman into bed. I was frozen for only a moment; such was my shock that this formidable, nearly invincible appearing man came from someone so fragile.

She groaned and mumbled something incoherent as he got her top half onto the bed with a grunt of effort. She was dead weight and it made her harder to handle from the way she seemed to come out of unconsciousness to struggle.

I didn't say a word. I moved into the room and lifted her legs as he carried her upper body, helping to lift her on to the bed.

He looked at me with surprise and then anger before muttering something unintelligible.

"I'm fine, honey," she was mumbling over and over, shaking her head against the pillow. Then she appeared to notice me through her drunken haze. "Who're you?" she slurred, looking at me through bleary eyes.

I looked to Axel wondering how he'd want to answer that.

"She's my girl, Ma," he responded impatiently.

"Nice to meet you, ma'am," I answered awkwardly, my eyes darting to Axel's and offering what I hoped was a reassuring smile.

"Ma'am," she sighed, throwing her head back against the pillow. "I like her, Axel," she laughed to herself. "It's 'bout time you settled down."

"Ma," he sighed in exasperation, all while stroking her hair back from her forehead with a tenderness that made my heart hurt.

Then with a sudden groan, she leaned over and threw up all over the side of the bed missing Axel's boots by inches as he jerked back.

"Fuck," he muttered, looking up to the ceiling as though searching for divine intervention. His lack of surprise made it clear this wasn't the first time this had happened.

"I drank too much," his mother groaned.

"Ya think?" Axel grumbled, seeming unclear where to start with the mess.

I darted from the room on a mission. I found the bathroom, a washcloth and a glass of water.

When I returned, I moved to the side of the bed that didn't have fresh vomit on it and sat carefully on its edge. I wiped her slack mouth with the washcloth and tried to coax her up to drink some water.

"Did I throw up on you?" she asked, seeming genuinely concerned.

"No," I replied quietly with a small shake of my head.

She threw her head back and sighed. "That's good."

I looked over to Axel who still hadn't looked me in the eye.

"I'll get a trash can," I murmured rising from my seat on the bed.

He grabbed hold of my arm as I moved to pass him. "You are not cleaning up my ma's puke. Go outside and sit your ass on the bike," he growled.

I looked at his grip on my arm and then up to his eyes that were filled with too many emotions to name. But I recognized one, shame. I wasn't about to let him feel embarrassed about this. Not with me.

"That's exactly what I'm going to do," I replied quietly. "I know something about having parents you're not proud of," I murmured, looking over at his mother who was now completely passed out, with her mouth hanging open. "I'm going to help you get this cleaned up. I know you'd do the same for me," I added with conviction.

He looked at me intently for a few moments before he swallowed audibly. "Fine," he groused as though it pained him to give in, again.

Together, we cleaned up the room relatively quickly. Once done in the bedroom, I started on the dishes in the sink. The house wasn't in that bad a shape given the circumstances. I had a million questions about how often she drank like this, what she'd been like when the boys were young, but I held my tongue, sensing it wasn't the time.

"Come on, Soph, we've been here long enough," he grumbled from behind me as I was drying one of the plates I'd washed.

I nodded in understanding that he'd want to get out of there. "Is she…" my voice trailed off as I looked toward the bedroom down the hall. "Will she be okay by herself?"

He snorted. "She'll sleep it off like she always does."

"Okay," I replied, watching his jerky movements as he shoved his jacket on. He was well and truly pissed off.

"I'll drop you home," his deep voice rumbled as I followed him outside the house.

I eyed him steadily for a moment, trying not to be deterred by his curtness.

"You don't want to eat?" I asked lightly, following his long, angry strides to his bike. It was well past lunch and I was starving. We had some time yet; Kat had texted not long ago saying Mad was down for a nap.

Aggravated, he rubbed his hand through his hair and looked off to the side, helmet in hand. "My ma always puts me in a shit mood. I should just drop you home. Take care of some shit," he shrugged. I didn't miss the inference that said 'shit' would be done alone.

He was trying to protect me like he always did, even from himself.

I snorted. "When are you not in a shit mood?" I teased. "You're like a growling bear half the time but somehow I still love you," I smiled before realizing what I'd said.

His demeanor shifted entirely from something foreboding to a different kind of intensity altogether. He moved into my space, his large hands cupping both sides of my face. "What did you just say?" his voice was a hoarse murmur as his thumbs traced the outline of my lips.

"You heard me," I whispered.

"I want to hear it again," he growled. "So I can say it back," he added, his words making my heart pound.

"I love you," I repeated, wrapping my arms around his neck.

"And I love you, baby," he replied, his full lips covering mine. "You couldn't have picked a better day to tell me that," he said between kisses.

I pulled back slightly, looking up into his face. "I'm glad. Because you know, if anyone knows we're not defined by who we came from, it's me," I assured him.

He pressed his forehead to mine. "I know. Let's get the fuck out of here."

I nodded as he took my hand, leading me to his bike. "I'm starving. I'll even eat Mariachi's." I wrinkled my nose and he chuckled.

"Shit, you must really be hungry. All right, darlin', hop up." He nodded with a grin that warmed me from the inside out.

I wrapped myself around him as we roared off, giving him my support by holding him close as we put his past behind us, kicking up dust as we barreled toward our future.

Chapter Thirteen

"What're we havin'?" Ryker asked enthusiastically, already poking through the Chinese takeout we'd picked up for a late dinner. I seriously needed to learn how to cook. We ate take out entirely too much. He'd let himself in as we were getting ready to eat. Rather than be annoyed that Ry had a key, I thought it was sort of sweet.

"We're not having anything," Axel retorted, tossing a bottle cap at Ryker when he'd begun rummaging.

I laughed at the brothers' antics and got Ry a plate. "Geez, at least someone is nice to me around here," Ry winked, dropping a swift kiss to my temple.

"I think we're going to watch something if you want to hang out, Ry," I offered, plopping on one of the two huge sofas that made up the living room.

"Thanks, sis, but I got plans," he replied, stuffing a huge bite of chow Mein in his mouth.

Ryker usually had 'plans' and they usually involved a woman. Lots of women.

"Uh huh," I nodded with a lifted brow.

"You got that run for Cole tomorrow, bro," Axel reminded him gruffly.

"Yeah, yeah," Ryker mumbled, scooping Mad up from his play mat and making a ridiculous face at him. He always had Maddox giggling.

"Say good night to Mad," I smiled, taking Maddox out of his uncle's arms.

"Night, bud," Ry replied.

"Night, little man," Axel added, coming over to move his large hand over Mad's head and back.

I took my time putting Maddox down, giving the two brothers some time to talk. I could tell Axel had more to say and probably didn't want to reprimand Ry in front of me.

When I headed back out to the living room, Ryker was on his way out. "Thanks for the grub." He shot me a chin lift, his mouth still full of food.

"Have fun, Ry," I waved.

We soon heard the boom of his bike and its resonating rumble as it took off down the road.

"He can be such a little shit," Axel shook his head, though his tone held no anger.

I continued to eat without reply, knowing he wasn't really expecting one.

"Mad go down okay?"

"Yeah," I nodded.

"He might sleep a little better with a real crib in there," he hinted.

It wasn't the first time he'd pressed me about officially moving in. It wasn't that I didn't want to. I did. I just wanted to take my time getting there. Part of me worried that this was all too good to be true. I couldn't really have it all...could I?

"He might," I answered vaguely.

"What do you wanna watch?" he sighed, claiming the remote.

"Vikings?" I asked with a cocked brow, knowing that's what he wanted. It was still the only show we could agree on.

"Sounds good," he nodded.

"You okay?" I asked quietly.

He turned to look at me, seeming to consider his response for a minute. "Yeah," he shrugged.

I continued to watch him out of the corner of my eye.

"What do you want to know?" he grumbled, running a hand over his beard.

"What do you mean?" I asked with my best innocent expression.

He snorted. "You're practically in pain over there holding in your questions."

I blushed at how well he could read me. "I do have a few," I admitted cautiously. "Where's your dad?"

"Getting right to it huh?" he chuckled darkly.

I shrugged, biting my lip.

"In jail," Axel replied without emotion as he sipped his beer.

I tried to hide my surprise – that certainly wasn't the answer I'd been expecting. "For what?" I asked carefully.

His eyes remained on the screen as I turned to face him, awaiting his answer. "Attempted murder," he answered curtly.

I waited for him to elaborate but he didn't, and I wasn't sure how hard to push. It wasn't just a lack of desire to share – no, this ran deeper, something akin to shame. I'd do anything to rid him of that baggage even if it meant sharing some of my own.

"My mother locked me in my room every night for a month," I blurted before I could stop myself.

That got his attention. "What?" he demanded, muting the TV.

"She…wanted me to lose weight," I stammered. "She started me on this insane diet. I was only in middle school." I explained pensively, uncomfortable that he was eyeing me with such intensity. "I would creep down to the kitchen to try to sneak food after dinner. She caught me." I shrugged, my cheeks heating. "So she locked me in my room every night after dinner until I lost the weight," I murmured. "It was never about how smart I was or what I could make of myself." I sighed, running a hand through my hair. "It was all about my looks. I needed to be beautiful to attract a high pedigree husband." I snorted.

"And what did you want?" he asked, his deep voice cutting through my jumbled thoughts.

I turned to him in surprise. No one had ever asked me that. "No one's ever asked me that," I whispered my thought aloud.

"Well, I'm askin'," he answered.

That right there that was why Axel was so life altering for me. From the moment I'd set eyes on him, it had been about what I wanted. He'd been the first choice I'd made that was for me alone.

"I want to teach," I told him. "Always have. Growing up, my teachers they saved my life," I shared as he pulled my legs into his lap.

His large hands moved up and down my legs in a rhythmic fashion that soothed me. "I'm sure you'd be great at that, babe," his deep voice rumbled.

"Someday," I agreed. "I graduated with a double

major, economics to please my parents and education for me. It wouldn't take long to get my credential. But now with Mad…" I trailed off. "I'm not sure when I'll have time."

"We'll make time," he assured me. "If it's what you want," he added.

My mouth opened and closed a few times as I struggled with what to say. It felt like my heart was full to bursting; his words meant so much to me. "Thanks, honey," I managed, squeezing his hand.

Silence fell over us as we continued to watch the show on mute. The battle scene was reaching its climax, the drama no less intense despite the silence.

"It was my ma." His deep voice cut through the air like a whip.

I turned to him in shock. "What?"

He nodded. "My pop, he was a bastard, the likes you've never seen. He drank like a fish, cheated on her with every woman who flashed her tits and gambled away every cent he earned." He made a sound of disgust.

I sat enthralled and horrified as he finally began to share. I was afraid to even breathe too loudly for fear he'd stop.

"He hit her, hit me and Ry 'til I got old enough to stop him."

I nodded silently, so much coming together for me with his explanation. The violence juxtaposed with his fiercely protective nature. He'd been an enforcer all his life – protecting his brother and his mother.

"One night, I wasn't home. Ry wasn't big enough—" his voice was so hoarse with anger and emotion I could barely make out the words. "He knocked Ry out, nearly killed Ma." He shook his head as though to rid himself of the nightmare. "So he's rotting in jail. It's the next best thing to six-feet under," he murmured, the venom in his words louder than any sound could be.

I waited silently, wanting him to get it all out and knowing he wasn't done.

"The thing that fuckin' killed me," he continued quietly as his eyes stared unseeing at the TV, "was that my ma seemed to miss the bastard." He snorted. "She never recovered after he got locked up. She'd always been a drinker, but once he went away, it got ten times worse." He shook his head. "Having us, having her fucking life, it wasn't enough for her. So in the end, I lost them both, if I ever had them at all," he admitted.

I tried hard to school my expression since I knew the last thing he wanted was my pity. Now empathy that was something I could give him – on some level at least.

"Ry was lucky to have you," I offered quietly.

"I wish you woulda had someone to protect you," he replied as I curled myself deeper into his body. "Did Sal know how bad things were for you?"

I shook my head. My brother had taken off as soon as he could have. I often wished he'd checked in with me more – tried to keep in better touch, but I knew he already felt horrible guilt about it.

"Why didn't you tell him? You could have gotten out of that shit so much earlier," he demanded, frustrated.

I put a hand to his chest, leaning away to look at him. "It was all I knew," I defended. "I didn't have the same ability as Sal to think bigger. He always seemed to know there was something else out there for him, something better. For me, it just took longer to realize. In the end,

I'd like to think the timing was perfect since it gave me Maddox – and you."

His expression softened as he reached a hand up to stroke my neck with his thumb. "You're right, baby," his deep voice rumbled.

"Mad won't have grandparents on either side," I whispered, the regret evident in my voice. "Does your mom even know about him?"

Axel snorted. "If she sobered up long enough to understand, I'd tell her. But no, she doesn't. Mad won't have grandparents." He shrugged as though the thought didn't faze him. "What he'll have are two parents who love him and protect him. Far more than either of us had," he continued as a familiar warmth spread in my belly. I'd never known the sensation until Axel came into my life.

"Yeah," I agreed, smiling into his earnest eyes.

"We'll give him everything he needs, plus a sibling or two," he grinned.

My eyes widened in shock. "Uh, what?" I stammered.

"Fuck, yes," he nodded with no hesitation. "Not only should Mad have a brother or sister, but I got robbed of seeing you pregnant the last time," he explained, his large hand splayed on my flat belly. "I want to see you get round. I want to feel the baby kick." His lips moved to my neck and my entire body melted. "I want to learn which parts of you are the most sensitive," he continued, his lips moving over my skin. "I want all of it. You gonna give me that?" His tongue traced the outline of my jaw.

In that moment, I would have promised him just about anything.

"Y-yeah," I breathed, my fingers finding purchase in his thick hair. "But not anytime soon," I found the sanity to add.

He chuckled against my skin. "No, baby, we have our hands full. But you know what they say – practice makes perfect."

I squealed as he hauled me up over his shoulder and strode to the bedroom.

I'd say we were pretty close to perfection already.

******

Maddox and I were at the club the following evening while Ax and the guys met. I assumed we'd be leaving soon since it was nearly bedtime for Mad. We'd been spending a lot of time there over the past few weeks since Axel refused to ever leave us home alone. I started keeping a few key baby items there rather than dragging everything around. The sight of the Pack' N Play against the wall in the main room still made me giggle. To their credit, none of the guys said anything about it but rather seemed to enjoy having the kids around. Gracie was another frequent visitor.

Maddox had changed in the time we'd been in Hawthorne. Aside from just getting bigger and learning new things every day, he was much more adaptable. He was now used to sleeping in all kinds of places. He was comfortable being passed around and being cared for by many different people. I loved the change. He had a huge extended family and he seemed to be embracing it as much as I was.

I heard the rumble of a bike and soon Mack walked in. "Hey, girl." He gave me a chin lift as he ambled toward where the guys were meeting.

I smiled and gave him a little wave, turning my attention back to Mad. It wasn't long after that I heard the roar of what sounded like several motorcycles. I didn't think much of it until three men appeared in the doorway with Black Riders cuts on.

My eyes widened with panic. I had absolutely nothing good to associate with that insignia. Plus, I knew Axel would have told me if this was an expected visit.

I snatched Maddox up and pressed him close to my chest. My whole body began to shake as that night with Aron and Jeb came rushing back. I was afraid to move as the three men assessed me without emotion.

Cal strode out a moment later, no doubt having heard the bikes. His blue eyes gleamed as he took in the three men in his club. His gaze then shot to me and he didn't hesitate. "Axel!" he barked loudly. Axel appeared not a moment later, his entire posture stiffening when he saw the men who'd crossed their door. "See to your woman," Cal instructed.

Axel's head swung toward me as he took in my shaking frame and huge eyes. His long legs ate up the space between us. "Babe," he began, his tone low.

"T-take Mad," I whispered, my teeth practically chattering.

He did as I asked, hoisting our son into his arms, his eyes never leaving mine. Mad grinned up at his daddy, oblivious to the tension.

"What's wrong with her?" one of the Black Riders asked, his tone confused and almost accusatory.

Axel turned to him with fire in his eyes. "What's wrong with her?" he growled. "What's wrong with her is that fucker Aron helped kidnap her and terrorized her in a motel room until she escaped. That's what the fuck is wrong with her!" he shouted.

The man held up his hands in a placating gesture. "Sorry, brother, I didn't realize she was your woman. I didn't know who she was," he tried to explain.

"I'm not your brother," Axel spat.

"Axel, take your family home," Cal ordered brusquely. "Now."

Axel wasn't happy with the order. His chest heaved as he glared daggers at the three men filling the doorway.

The tension was palpable as my anxiety grew more pronounced.

"Ax, man," Cole's voice suddenly filled the space. I hadn't even realized he was here. "If it were my woman, I'd feel the same fucking way and you'd tell me the same thing. You've got too much skin in this game. Take your girl home. Trust your brothers. We've got your back," he assured him.

After a moment, Axel nodded reluctantly. "Yeah, man." He wrapped his arm around my shoulders and led us past the men and to the truck parked out front. He opened the door for me, guiding me with his large hand to crawl in while he still held our son. "Seatbelt," he commanded, moving around the other side to get Maddox strapped in his seat.

He didn't say a word the entire drive back home. His demeanor didn't invite conversation and I was so wrapped up in my own thoughts that I didn't press him. I did have the presence of mind to wish he'd offer some form of comfort, no matter how small. Tension poured off him in waves and I wondered what exactly had him so keyed up.

The air had a new chill when we pulled up and carried Mad inside. Fall was officially upon us. I looked up at the sky wistfully hoping we'd have the kind of holiday season

I'd dreamed about since I was a child. The kind filled with laughter and love – not appearances and forced emotion.

"I'll take him," I murmured in our darkened entryway, reaching out for a sleepy Maddox. Axel handed him over without a word.

"Sweet boy," I murmured into his soft hair that was coming in thicker every day. "You're ready for bed, aren't you?" I talked softly to him as I carried him into the office and got him changed. He had his last bottle at the club so he was ready to roll. I looked around the office wondering if it was time to convert it into a nursery. Axel had asked me several times, when was I ready to make it his room? When was I ready to call his place ours?

Maybe it was time to take the plunge.

I swayed back and forth, humming an unnamed melody to Mad as his eyes drooped. I knew I could put him down but holding him calmed my frazzled nerves. Seeing those men, those jackets, had brought back so many unwanted memories and emotions. Then there was Axel. He was seriously pissed and I wasn't sure I had the capacity to deal with his emotion as well as mine. Not right then anyway.

"Night, sweetie," I cooed softly, placing my sleeping baby in his crib. I smoothed his hair back from his beautiful face and slipped out of the room in search of my man.

I found him pacing the master bedroom like a caged beast. I eyed him warily as he pulled on his hair and looked ready to break down a wall or two.

"What's the matter?" I asked quietly when it didn't seem like he was going to stop any time soon.

He turned to glare at me, the venom in his expression taking me by surprise. Axel had never directed anger at me. Frustration? Irritation? Sure. But nothing like the feral rage I saw now.

"I should be there," he growled by way of reply.

"Where?" I asked, confused.

"At the club! Not fucking playing house!" he roared.

I took a step back, reeling from his anger and the bite of his words. It was a minute before I could even respond.

"Is that what we're doing? Playing house?" I shot back through numb lips.

He threw up his hands. "That's not what I fucking meant!" he hollered.

"Keep your voice down!" I hissed.

"I have to go." He shook his head, grabbing his cut off the chair. "I can't deal with this shit."

I wondered which shit he meant specifically but couldn't bear to ask for fear of what he'd say. I fought fiercely to battle down my own temper. To bite back the demand of where my feelings played into all this. He was obviously warring with himself over something and this wasn't the time.

"Talk to me," I asked quietly, moving a step closer.

He groaned, throwing his head back to look at the ceiling. "I'm not a man who should be talking about fucking feelings," he huffed. He held up his fists, clenched so tight his knuckles were white. "I use these – it's who I am," he grit out. "The club needs me to be that and I can't be that when I have to take care of you," he shot out, leveling me with a frustrated stare.

Holy hell, ouch. It was as though he verbally socked me in the gut. My eyes pooled with tears at his harsh words.

"Well, please, don't do me any favors," I murmured hoarsely.

"Fuck! I'm no good like this. I'm leaving," he muttered,

moving past me.

I stood shocked in the sudden quiet, feeling like I'd just been through a hurricane and was left with the wreckage.

I heard his bike start up in the garage and the tears filling my eyes spilled over and down my cheeks. I swiped at them angrily, frustrated he could decimate me so suddenly. He demanded time and time again that I let him take care of us, yet he threw that back in my face.

Well, screw that shit.

I pulled myself together and picked up the phone, calling the only person I wanted in that moment who also happened to be the last person I should share this with.

Chapter Fourteen

Sal was quiet on the drive down the mountain. We'd taken Mad's car seat out of Axel's truck and without a word he'd installed it and helped me with my things. I felt guilty for disturbing Maddox but there was no way I was waiting for Axel to come back – whenever the hell that was.

If he didn't want to be burdened with us, then I was more than happy to let him have his house back. That was what I was telling myself anyway.

I looked out the window lost in thought as we drove. Sal didn't press and allowed me my space.

We pulled up to Sal and Kat's new place. They'd moved in a few months ago wanting more space for the baby. Their ranch-style place was close to Wes and Connie's and had four bedrooms, plenty of space.

Kat swept in quietly when we walked in and led me into their nursery. They'd just started decorating but had a crib already up that I set Maddox in. He immediately went back to sleep.

"You can stay in here," she murmured, ushering me to their guest room.

"Little different than the last time I dropped on

your doorstep," I smiled dryly, looking around the neat room with a queen-sized bed. When I'd first arrived in Hawthorne, I'd shown up on Sal's doorstep without warning. He had a two bedroom house back then and the second bedroom was in no shape for a guest.

I looked over at my brother who leaned in the doorway, his dark eyes assessing. "Sal, you're so grown up," I teased lightly as I set my overnight bag down on the bed.

"I'll go get some towels," Kat offered and I knew she was just giving us a minute.

"I can't believe I'm gonna say this but whatever that idiot did, I'm sure he didn't mean it," Sal muttered. "Want to talk about it?"

"What is it with you two anyway?" I asked, sitting on the end of the bed warily.

He sighed in resignation. "We've had some dust-ups over the years," he admitted with a shrug. "We prospected at the same time all those years ago. I was an outsider and he'd known most of the guys all their lives. He didn't trust me for a long-ass time." He chuckled wryly. "I guess it went both ways. We've gotten a lot better over the years, but I guess when you came back into town and I saw his reaction to you – well, it struck a nerve. It was less about him though; I admit that was part of it – and more about how you'd grown up. I didn't think any of the guys would be a good match. Especially when I wasn't gonna let anyone take advantage of you," he explained.

"You're a good big brother," I replied softly.

A look of guilt swept over his face. "Shit, Soph, I could have been so much better," he grumbled shaking his head. "I shouldn't have left you. That was some fucking selfish bullshit."

"Sal, you were eighteen. You're supposed to be selfish at eighteen," I protested.

"Still," he lamented. "But, Soph, what I said about any of the guys taking advantage. It was clear pretty damn quick that wasn't Axel's agenda. Not with you," he shook his head. "He loves you and he loves Maddox," he said firmly.

I looked down at my hands and the tears pooled again in my eyes. "I know he does," I shrugged, biting my lip and trying not to do the whole ugly-cry thing. I was surprised Sal was venturing this far into the emotional zone. I didn't want to scare him away. "He just...tonight he was so mad," I whispered. "He made me feel like Mad and I are holding him back from what he wants to be doing, like we're a burden. I didn't understand where any of that was coming from or why he was so angry. He's fought so hard to make me feel like he wants to take care of us but then his actions tonight said otherwise."

"Shit," Sal muttered and sighed, coming to sit awkwardly next to me. "I'm sure that sucked," he acknowledged. "And I'll gladly pound him if you want."

I chuckled on a sob and shook my head before he continued.

"Ax has never had a woman – not one he cared for like you, Soph," he sighed. "It's an adjustment. It was for me, too. It's like two sides of yourself warring all of a sudden. That's my guess of what might be going on anyway. Doesn't make it right but there it is," he shrugged as Kat returned bearing a cup of tea.

"Everything okay?" she asked.

I nodded though it really wasn't. "I think I just want to go to bed. Thanks for letting me stay. Sorry for imposing."

"It's no trouble. You guys are welcome any time," Kat rushed to say. I could tell she wanted to ask for details but restrained herself. "Let us know if you two need anything."

"I will, thanks."

"Night, Soph, it'll work out," Sal assured me, clasping the crown of my head with affection before they left me to my thoughts.

I looked at my phone. He hadn't even called, didn't even realize we were gone. I winced, thinking how freaked he'd be if he didn't know where we were. That wasn't fair to him. No matter how mad and confused I was, I didn't want him to worry. I shot him a brief text.

At my brother's. We're safe.

I turned off my ringer and quietly got ready for bed, crawling under the unfamiliar covers. It took me a long time to find sleep. I tossed and turned, Axel's anger haunting me even after I'd fallen asleep.

There was a faint tapping that grew louder as I roused, feeling groggy. I wasn't even sure how long I'd been sleeping.

"Soph," Sal's deep quiet voice cut through the darkness.

"Is Maddox okay?" I asked groggily.

"Yeah. But Axel's here. I told him he can't come in but he's pretty damn determined."

"What time is it?" I rasped, sitting up and wiping my hair back from my face.

"Two."

"Fantastic," I muttered. "Sorry, Sal." I felt bad that they'd taken me in and were now being awoken by a perpetually moody Axel Black.

He snorted. "I had money he'd show up by now. Don't worry about it." He waved me off.

"But Kat," I protested, knowing how tired she was these days.

"She'd sleep through a fuckin' parade. She's out; otherwise, I'd be out there having more than words with your man."

I didn't doubt that was true.

"I don't want to put you in the middle of this but can you send him home?" I asked, my voice sounding small in the dim light.

"I'm not going anywhere," Axel's voice cut through the night with booming conviction.

"Fuck, man, I told you to stay out there," Sal bit out.

"And I told you to stay the fuck out of it," Axel growled. "She's your sister. I get it. But she's my woman and that's my son in there." He jerked a finger toward the nursery.

"Yeah and you're acting like a fucking jackass," Sal snarled.

"Sal, fuck, man, don't make me remind you of all the shit you pulled on Kat," Axel appealed to my brother with a sincere effort toward peace. "'Cause I took care of your girl while you were gone and I didn't fuckin' judge you for that shit."

There was a heavy pause and I honestly couldn't tell which way this would go.

"You're right," Sal agreed, shocking the hell out of me. "I was no saint." He shook his head. "I get some of what you're going through. But she's my little sister, man. Anytime she turns up on my doorstep, I'll take her in. Don't cross a line where I don't let you in," he warned.

"I won't," Axel agreed.

"All right, I'm headed to bed," my brother said gruffly. "Keep it down. If you wake up Kat, I'll kick your ass out."

He shot a look at Axel though I could tell most of his anger had left him.

I crossed my arms over my chest and glared at both of them.

"Good luck, dude," Sal muttered, slipping from the room.

"If my brother won't kick you out, I will," I hissed toward Axel after the door had been quietly shut.

He didn't answer me but clicked the light off instead. I heard the sound of his boots dropping one by one to the floor with heavy thunks that ricocheted off the walls. When I heard the sound of his belt and jeans falling to the ground, I stared at him with wide eyes through the dark room.

"What the hell are you doing?" I demanded incredulously.

"Babe, we're gonna fight; I don't know much but I know that," he muttered. "I'm an angry motherfucker and you're as sweet as you are stubborn."

"I am not stubborn," I argued.

He chuckled as I glared.

"We'll fight," he continued as he climbed up onto the bed. I scooted away indignantly. "But baby, you're mine. You sleep under our roof or I find the one you're under."

"Not if you're going to fight like hell for us and then when you get pissed make me feel like a burden," I argued.

"You're never a burden," he replied, his voice tired but sincere. "I'm just not used to fixing things by talkin'," he explained. "It's always been with my fists. When those fucks showed up at the club, I've never felt so torn. I didn't want you out of my sight but I also wanted to let them know who the hell they'd answer to if they stepped out of line."

"So you chose to be with me and regretted it?" I asked confused and hurt.

"All I regretted was feeling like I didn't do enough to protect you by letting everyone else handle business that I felt was mine."

"That sounds like it's more about what you needed than what I needed," I pointed out.

There was a charged pause while he took that in.

"Fuck, you're right," he admitted.

He sounded so surprised by that realization and so tired that I softened some.

"I love you and I swear I'm tryin'," he added as I heard the pillow rustle under his head. I knew his gaze had turned to me and I was glad the room was dark. Those eyes always made me melt and I needed to stay strong here. "There's nothing in this goddamned world I want more than you and Mad. Taking care of you, protecting you – it gives me a purpose like I've never known. Anything I said to make you feel otherwise was said in anger and was complete and utter bullshit," he swore.

I took that in for a minute.

"Okay," I murmured. I believed him. I knew we both had to operate on a learning curve; this whole thing was new to both of us.

"Okay?" he asked, his voice relieved.

"Yeah," I answered. "I just think – well, I feel like you're censoring yourself for my benefit. If Mad and I force you to change too much, this will never work," I shook my head. "I think what we need is some balance," I surmised.

"All right," he agreed. "I also think we need to have some goddamned fun, Soph. Let me take you away for a night. Sal and I already talked about it. You and I need some time, just us."

"Leave Mad?" I questioned nervously.

"With your brother and Kat," he interjected. "One night, Soph, it'll be good for us. He loves them both, he'll be fine."

"I don't know," I fretted. I'd never left Maddox overnight.

He reached over, pulling me close to his chest. "You know I'd never suggest it if I didn't know he'd be well taken care of. I don't regret the way we ended up here. I fucking love our life. But I never did the whole dating thing. Never wanted to. But with you, well, I want to spend time with you. Alone," he pressed.

I giggled quietly at the urgency in his tone.

"Yeah, okay," I agreed. "What did you have in mind?"

Chapter Fifteen

I found myself regretting sharing that I'd never been camping.

Growing up in Manhattan and having parents who were positively repelled by the outdoors, my closest experiences with nature had been Central Park.

Axel hadn't liked that so much.

When he suggested a night away, this hadn't been exactly what I'd had in mind but I was determined to roll with it.

The campground he'd brought us to was gorgeous, surrounded by pine trees and amazing rock formations. It was fairly private with only a few other campsites occupied. I appreciated the smell and the sense of calm.

What I did not appreciate was the fact it was outside. As in, sleeping outside. As in, no bathroom anywhere close.

Axel had set up the small tent and bedroll that had been hooked to the back of his bike within mere minutes.

"Done this before?" I asked with a quirk of my brow.

"A time or two," he nodded, not elaborating.

"I think you can take that thing off now," I gestured to the shoulder holster he'd worn since we'd left Hawthorne, and when I thought about it, most of the time when we weren't at home.

"Nope." he shook his head simply.

"We're in the middle of nowhere," I protested.

He shrugged, telling me without words that didn't matter to him. I knew even if we were in a high-class hotel somewhere, it'd be the same thing.

I sat on a picnic bench, swinging my legs, watching him work.

"You gonna get up off that sweet ass and help me out?" he demanded with a grin.

"I'll make dinner," I offered with a shrug.

He tried to hide his apprehension but didn't succeed.

"What?" I demanded.

"Uh, babe, you burn macaroni and cheese." He replied, biting back a smile as my eyes narrowed. "I didn't even think that was possible," he added with a stifled chuckle.

"Fine, then you can cook," I snapped.

"I've got my hands full with you, don't I?" He grinned, seeming absurdly pleased.

"You don't have to have your hands full of anything," I retorted, crossing my arms over my chest.

"Christ, what crawled up your ass?" he chortled. He moved close, his large hands moving to my hips. "Why don't you tell me what's got you so pissed off all of a sudden?" his large body moved in between my legs, effectively caging me in.

I looked everywhere but at him as I felt him stare intently at me. He wasn't going to let this go.

"Well?" he prompted.

"There's so many things I can't do! I can't even cook macaroni! That was the only time I've tried to cook it and I couldn't even do it without cooking the noodles to mush."

He took my chin, forcing me to look at him as his expression warmed. "You want to cook for me?" he asked with a smile.

"Well...yeah," I shrugged, my face flaming.

He leaned in, kissing me softly. "I'll eat your mushy macaroni anytime, darlin'" he winked.

I wrinkled my nose but bit back a smile in response.

"There's a few things you can't do," he allowed with a shrug. "There are so many things you're amazing at. You know that. So you can't cook?" he shrugged.

"I still can't drive," I mumbled.

"I'll give you another lesson when we get home," he agreed.

I scoffed. "You practically had a heart attack with the last one!"

"I'll get better; we both will," he replied and I knew he meant more than just the driving lesson.

"Yeah," I murmured, taking in how close he was. I pulled on his shirt to draw him closer.

I saw him visibly swallow as his eyes darkened. His phone rang then, breaking the sexual tension between us. "Yeah?" he asked gruffly, his eyes still locked on mine. "Oh, yeah?" he asked, a smile breaking out across his face. "That's awesome. I'll let her know. Yeah." He listened for a moment, his hand high on my thigh. "Good to hear, man. Will do, later." He shut his phone off as I cocked my head to the side, curious. "That was Sal; Mad's doing great."

"Oh good," I breathed a sigh of relief, looking up at the trees and wilderness around us.

"Did you camp much as a kid?" I thought to ask.

He snorted, delivering me a quick kiss before he moved back over to the stove to continue making dinner. "My parents never took us anywhere. I've always loved the outdoors," he explained. "I feel like I can really breathe out here."

I thought back on the house where he'd grown up and understood why he'd feel that way.

"Yeah, I can see that," I agreed softly. "You gonna teach this city girl some new tricks?" I teased.

He turned to me, his eyes heated. "Hell, yes," he answered without hesitation.

******

"I have to pee," I whispered, for what felt like the tenth time that night.

"No, you don't," Axel muttered through the darkness of our tent.

We'd had a campfire dinner and some beers; I'd even peed in the woods for the first time with moderate success. Axel stood with his back to me, giving me crap the entire time about making sure I didn't fall over or let anything bite me on the ass.

Then we turned in.

At first I liked the tent and snuggling close to Axel, especially the snuggling part. But the moment we said goodnight and I realized there wasn't a bathroom nearby I felt like I had to pee. I'd already gotten up once to try, dragging Axel with me.

"I do," I insisted.

"You don't; it's just in your head, babe, would you relax?" he mumbled, rolling over and pulling me close. We'd opened up two sleeping bags, one for the bottom and one serving as a quilt.

I let the silence wash over us for a little while, taking

in the night sounds of the wilderness in a way I'd never experienced. It was beautiful, peaceful even. My mind just couldn't seem to rest.

"What's the plan here anyway?" I whispered after a time.

"The plan is to sleep and not go piss in the woods again," he grumbled.

I socked him lightly in the shoulder. "You know what I mean. I keep thinking about my father. He's been quiet. Too quiet." I shared my anxiety through the darkness.

He sighed and rolled to his back, scrubbing a hand over his face. "I know. I have a plan. I just need you to trust me and let things play out for now. Do you think you can do that?"

"Why can't you tell me the plan?" I asked with a knitted brow.

He sighed, feigning patience. "Because it's not ready," he answered simply.

What the heck did that mean?

"What the heck does that mean?" I voiced my question aloud.

Axel shifted beside me, pulling me close as his mouth moved to my neck. "Trust me."

Even though I wanted to know what he was thinking, I trusted him implicitly. Something, I realized I'd never felt for another person in my life.

"You're the best friend I've ever had," I told him, feeling extraordinarily brave in the darkness.

He kissed me. "Oh, baby, we're a lot more than friends."

"Of course we are. But I never had true friends. People I could trust. I trust you with everything, even my life. You and Mad mean more to me than anyone else has in my entire life," I told him seriously, needing him to understand.

He pulled me close, as his breathing changed to something deeper. Something more ragged. What I'd said had touched something deep. I knew that.

His lips found mind in a desperate kiss, much different from the light fooling around we'd done earlier. I felt his hardness against my belly and answered with a soft moan. His hand lifted my shirt up and off, his mouth latching on to my nipple with vigor.

I surged into his mouth, wanting more, wanting everything. My hands caressed his bare chest before wandering lower. I stroked him over his boxers thinking not for the first time that he must be larger than normal. Surely this wasn't typical, was it? I certainly didn't have anything else to compare him to.

"Christ," he bit out as my hand explored the expanse of his hardness. He felt so smooth and yet hard, like velvet wrapped over steel.

His hands removed my pajama pants and underwear as we continued to explore each other's bodies.

His hand moved to my core, cupping lightly before his fingers honed in on their destination. In mere moments, he had me gasping and calling his name.

I was still recovering when I heard him rustling around in his discarded jeans and I realized he was putting on a condom.

My entire body hummed with anticipation.

Then his big body was between my legs, poised at my entrance that was slick and ready for him.

"Fuck," he breathed through labored breaths as he slid home. "Never felt anything like this, like you," he told me as he slid out and back in with a smooth glide.

He kissed me then, his tongue dueling with mine in a beautiful feud as his movements picked up.

I pulled him closer, loving the closeness and the feel of him inside me. His mouth moved back to my breast, sucking hard at my nipple as his hand slid down lower. The sensation from all pleasure points was nearly too much. It was so overwhelming.

Unbelievably, I felt that same wave build again, ready to overtake me if I let it.

"I'm close," he panted as his movements became less controlled – more out of sync. "You are too. I can feel it," he grunted.

I nodded, wrapping my legs that much tighter around him, wanting all of him, relishing being the cause of his loss of control.

Then I was there – hurtling over the edge, calling his name.

He surged inside me with desperation before he stilled, releasing a groan so sensual, I knew I'd remember it for the rest of my life.

He lay on me and in me for many long moments, our panting breaths the only sound to be heard. Then he slipped out and I sighed at the loss of him.

I heard him do something with the condom before his warm body returned to mine. "Come on, baby. Let's go get cleaned up," he murmured, kissing my neck.

I grinned up at him, raking my hands through his soft hair. I loved being with him like this – hell, I loved being with him any way I could get him. I'd never felt so safe to just be …me with anyone.

We dressed clumsily in the dim light of the little LED

flashlight he had and stepped into the cool air outside the tent. He shocked me by hoisting me up in his arms and striding us into the darkness.

"You don't have to carry me," I giggled, feeling practically buoyant.

"Yeah, I really do," he returned, breaking stride briefly to kiss me.

"Where are we going?"

"Bathrooms, babe," he replied.

I smacked his arm. "You didn't tell me there were bathrooms! Why have I been peeing in the woods?" I huffed while stifling a laugh. I wasn't mad, not really. I was too blissed out.

He chuckled. "Too far to walk for a piss, baby. Plus, it's part of the experience." He shrugged with a smile.

"You don't have to squat down in fear of something biting your ass. You can have the pissing in the woods experience all you want," I returned with an eye roll. "I'll stick to the bathrooms."

I could hear the smile in his voice as he replied, "Fair enough, darlin'. But you gotta pee in the middle of the night, you're on your own if you want to take a trek like this." He chuckled.

Dammit.

The showers were so much nicer than I expected and completely private at this late hour. We got naked again and took our time cleaning each other up.

It was playful and intimate, and like we were the only two people on Earth. By the time we made it back to our little tent in the woods, I was exhausted and yet content down to my bones.

He pulled me close, nuzzling the back of my neck as he

spooned me. "Night, baby."

"Night," I murmured.

As it turned out, I really liked camping after all.

Despite the fact that an hour later, I woke him up to take me to go pee in the woods.

Chapter Sixteen

I felt lighter, happier as we rolled back into Hawthorne the next morning. We'd taken our time getting up, stopping for breakfast on the way in. Axel had been right. We'd needed that time together. But I was now impatient to get back to Mad. We both were.

We rolled up to the house to swap the bike for the truck and headed into town to get our boy.

My phone rang as we were driving in and my heart's pace picked up as it always did when I saw an unfamiliar number flash across the screen.

"Who is it?" Axel asked brusquely.

"I don't know, should I answer it?" I asked him.

He gave a terse nod as I slid my finger over the screen. "Hello?"

"Sophie," my mother's rushed voice hit my ears.

I sat up straighter, shocked to hear from her and more so by her tone. Gone was her usual poise and standard calculated manner of speech.

"What do you want?" I replied coldly. "How did you get this number?"

Axel deftly pulled to the side of the road and mouthed to me to put it on speaker. I complied with shaky hands.

"I found it on your father's desk," she answered breathlessly. "I don't know how he got it but I think he's had it for a little while. He knows where you are." She delivered the news like a crushing blow.

I shot a look at Axel and he reached over and took my free hand, pulling it into his lap.

"Why can't he let this go?" I demanded furiously. "You both need to let me go!"

"I know." She shocked me by agreeing in a subdued voice. "This past year, Sophie, not knowing where you were – if you were safe. Knowing what we made you do." Her voice turned hoarse with an emotion I'd never heard in her before. "I just want you to be okay, Sophie. I don't want to lose both my children. I can't tell you how happy it makes me just to hear your voice."

I wished I could say the same.

"What does he want?" I asked, choosing to ignore her emotional plea. It was too little, too late.

"He's scaring me," she admitted. "He's a different man than I knew. I don't know what's driving it. He's convinced himself that you need to come home and marry Benjamin," she told me, referring to the senator's son that they'd tried to force on me so long ago.

I saw Axel visibly stiffen beside me at the very mention of Benjamin, as he made a motion that I should mute the phone.

"Just a minute," I told her, doing as he asked.

"You tell her you're already married, babe," he instructed.

"What?" I exclaimed.

"Not quite how I'd hoped to share my plans, but I knew all along we would need to play this card. Your brother and I have looked deep into the state of play with your father. You being spoken for in the eyes of the law puts a serious wrench in his plans. It might even make him back off altogether."

"But we're not married," I protested.

He leveled me with a heated look and I gasped, not quite ready to take in what he'd said without needing words.

"What about Mad?" I asked quietly.

He shook his head. "Don't mention him. I want him out of this. It sounds like she's still under the impression you didn't have him." My heart clenched at the very thought as I nodded in agreement.

"Mother," I began in a shaky voice as I took her off mute. "You need to tell Dad that I'm already married," I shared. "Whatever plans he has, he needs to keep me out of them."

Her intake of breath was more controlled than I would have expected. "When? Who?"

"It doesn't matter," I cut her off. "All you need to know – all I'd hope you'd care about – is that I'm safe and happy. Despite everything, I hope the same for you," I murmured. "Goodbye, Mother," I hung up swiftly, my hands moving shakily through my hair.

"Good job, baby," Axel praised me, pulling me forcefully into his lap so I straddled him.

"That sucked," I groused, burying my face into his neck and relishing the feel of his huge arms pulling me close and holding me tightly.

We sat there by the side of the road for several minutes before I pulled back to look him in the eye.

"Why didn't you tell me about this card you'd thought

we'd need to play?" I demanded. "That's a pretty big plan to keep to yourself."

He looked me in the eye, his hands moving to either side of my neck so his thumbs could stroke my lower lip. "Because I wanted to be able to propose to you properly," he shared. "I love you. I love Maddox. I want to have more babies with you. I want you to have my last name. I want to share my life with you. Marry me." His voice was thick with emotion.

My eyes filled with tears as I tried to grapple with my world tilting on its axis. "And it's not because you feel like you have to?" I hedged, admitting my worst fear aloud.

He grinned. "It's the only thing I could thank your father for, baby. He pushed up my timeline. This way I get a ring on your finger now rather than later. Marry me, Sophie," he whispered, pulling me closer still.

In the end, there was only one answer to that question. Despite everything, I'd never felt so sure of anything.

"Yes," I grinned at him before he took my mouth in a searing kiss.

His mouth opened up over mine, our tongues tangling as his fingers raked through my hair. My entire body liquefied as I pushed myself closer.

"I love you," I murmured against his mouth as our ragged breathing steamed up the windows.

"I love you, too, baby," he replied, pressing his forehead to mine. "If we weren't on the side of the road, we'd celebrate. Tonight," he promised, his eyes dark with desire.

I nodded, biting my lip in anticipation.

"Let's go get our boy."

"Yeah," I grinned.

Maddox greeted us with a gummy grin as Kat passed

him off to me.

"How'd he do?" I asked, kissing his chubby cheek and holding him close.

"Great," she beamed. "It's good practice for us." Sal came to wrap an arm around her shoulders.

"Not looking forward to changing all those diapers." He shook his head as she poked him in the side. "Fuck! How are they so rank? He hardly eats any solid food."

"Get ready," I teased.

"Did you guys have fun?" Kat asked.

I blushed furiously and looked up at Axel. "We did." He confirmed for me with a sly grin. "So much fun I got this girl to agree to marry me," he added proudly.

"No shit?" Sal smiled as Kat squealed.

"No shit," Axel nodded, accepting the handshake my brother extended.

I saw Kat look down at my bare ring finger curiously. Axel must have noticed as well. "The proposal I'd been planning got moved up due to an unexpected call on the way here from your mother," Axel replied, looking pointedly over at Sal.

"What?" Sal demanded, his eyes narrowing.

"It's time to throw down the gauntlet, man. Her father is fucking losing it. Thinks she's still gonna come back and marry that Benjamin kid." He shook his head in disbelief. "You knew I was already gonna propose, but I had her say we're already married."

"Good idea," Sal agreed. "You guys are gonna have to act quick then."

"Yeah," Axel nodded.

"What location can we pull together on such short notice?" Kat thought aloud.

"I know the exact spot," I put in, the image already clear in my mind.

Axel looked down at me in surprise. "What are you thinkin'?"

"Home," I grinned up at him. "The back deck would be perfect. It's big enough."

"I thought we'd all just go to Vegas," Sal admitted.

I shook my head. "I want to get married in the only place that's ever felt like home."

Axel's face warmed as he pulled me close. "You're okay with that? I figured you might want something more..." he searched for the right words.

I shrugged. "We can always do something more formal later if we want to. For now, I'm fine just having a big party as long as everyone can come on such short notice."

"I'll call the girls. We'll get everything planned for the day after tomorrow? That soon?" Kat verified.

"That soon," Axel nodded as my head spun.

She winked at me. "I love spontaneous marriages. I think they're good luck," Although engaged before their trip, she and Sal were married on a whim in Spain.

"Baby, don't get all spun out over this. Let Scar and Connie handle it. I don't want you stressed out," Sal told her.

"Okay, babe," she agreed, turning to me to roll her eyes.

"I saw that." Sal slapped her firmly on the ass.

The next twenty-four hours were a chaotic blur as the whole club worked to pull our wedding off. I was exhausted but so full of love for everyone around us that it gave me all the energy I needed.

The house was transformed in such a short time; I

wouldn't have thought it possible if I hadn't seen it myself. The living room became the reception area filled with flowers and tables and chairs. Kat even insisted on a dance floor. I had no idea how she got her hands on it.

The back deck had chairs lined up with a proper aisle down the center. We'd say our vows with the backdrop of evergreen and mountains.

The cake was ordered along with the food. Wes volunteered to handle the alcohol, which didn't surprise anyone in the least. We had our marriage license and Ryker got ordained online to marry us. It was all coming together.

During a quick trip to Vegas with the girls, I found a beautiful dress that fit like a glove. It was a gorgeous champagne color with a hint of a peach hue. Strapless with a tulle skirt, it was elegant and fun.

I'd meant it when I said I didn't need anything formal. If anything, this felt like the perfect way to marry the man of my dreams. In our home, doing what felt right to us without anyone else's expectations affecting our day.

In lieu of a formal bachelorette party, the girls were all coming over for drinks the night before the big day.

I'd put Mad down for the night and had fingers crossed that he stayed that way.

"I'll be back," Axel told me just as Connie, Scar, Ettie and I were settling in with our drinks in the living room.

"Back?" I asked, confused. I'd thought he was going to hang out with the guys until later.

"I have something to drop off," he replied mysteriously.

"Okaaay," I replied, intrigued by what he meant.

"Hank and Tag drew the short straws. They're on their way to watch over you ladies tonight," he chuckled.

Short straws indeed.

"Thank you, guys, so much for everything," I sighed wistfully. I looked around the living room, which was – despite a few small details – ready for my wedding day. White string lights hung throughout the room, basking the space in a warm glow, lighting the room. Axel was going to have to fight me not to keep it just like this.

"It was fun." Connie smiled, clinking her glass with mine. "You ready?" she asked with a grin.

"Yeah, I really am," I nodded. "It's fast but nothing about our relationship has been conventional so far; might as well stick with the trend." I laughed with a shrug.

"I think it's really freaking romantic," Ettie sighed. "The man is practically salivating to marry you as soon as possible. If you hadn't been the one talking to your mother, I'd have thought he made the whole thing up just for an excuse."

"Right?" I laughed. Axel had been...enthused by the prospect from the moment I'd agreed to marry him. It endeared him to me in a totally new way.

We sat around talking and laughing for a while before I heard the front door open. When Axel walked in with Jill and a sleepy Mason in tow, I almost fell out of my chair.

"Jill! Oh, my God!" I squealed, running over and throwing my arms around her. "How did you? When did you?" the words tumbled from my mouth as Axel chuckled.

"Your man here flew us out," she grinned, cocking her head toward Axel.

I turned to him with wide eyes brimming with sudden tears. "Babe," I tried to finish my thank you but the words were trapped in my throat.

He kissed me chastely, running a thumb over my tears.

"It was nothing, baby," he replied simply.

Maybe to him. To me it meant the world and he knew that.

"Thank you," I managed.

"You're welcome," he replied, stooping to touch his forehead with mine. "Now, I'll let you ladies have your fun. See you in a few hours, baby," he grinned, his eyes alight.

"Yeah," I beamed, watching my gorgeous man stride out of the room before turning my attention back to my friends.

We put Mason down in the guestroom where Jill would also spend the night. I was so beyond excited to see her I could barely stand it.

"Tim couldn't come?" I wondered aloud as I grabbed her a drink and we all got situated in the living room.

"No," she shook her head, not offering further details.

"Everything all right?" I asked carefully, not wanting to pry in front of the rest of the girls but wanting to make sure she was okay.

She shrugged. "It could be better but I'm not here to talk about me." She forced a smile. "I'm here to watch my best friend get married."

I eyed her thoughtfully for a minute, trying to decide if I should push the subject.

"Really, Soph," she added quietly. "I want to enjoy myself."

"Okay," I agreed, reaching over to grab her hand. I'd let it go but we were going to talk – and soon.

By the time Axel got back with Wes and Mack in tow, Ettie was passed out on the couch, Connie was dancing to music only playing in her head and Scarlet, Jill and I were immersed in a very serious conversation about the

TV show Scandal.

I'd taken it easy on the alcohol, not wanting to be hung over the next day, but I couldn't say the same for the rest of the ladies.

"Have fun?" Axel asked with a lifted brow, eyeing Connie with evident amusement.

"Yeah," I laughed as Wes sauntered over to his lady and twirled her, despite the lack of music. It was as though they were in their own little world as he grinned down at her with obvious adoration. Connie was a free spirit through and through. I loved that about her. Obviously, Wes did too.

Mack lifted Ettie off the couch and with a chin lift, carried her out to his truck. "Come on, ladies," Wes said to Scarlet and Connie. He draped an arm over his wife, and headed out with Scarlet following as they both called their goodbyes.

"I'll turn in," Jill announced, rising to stand a bit unsteadily on her feet.

"Okay," I hugged her close. "I'm so glad you're here," I murmured in her ear.

"Me too," she agreed, hugging me tightly.

"Come on, baby," Axel coaxed, quietly taking my hand. "Night, Jill," he called over his shoulder as he led me to our room.

"I think something's really wrong with Jill," I professed through the darkness after we crawled into bed. "She won't talk about it but she's always been dodgy about Tim."

"I'm sure she'll talk when she's ready," he replied, his fingers stroking through the hair at my temple. "For now, try not to worry about it. She wouldn't want you worried about her – not with the wedding."

"You're right. I'll try."

"You ready to be Mrs. Black?" I could hear the smile in his voice as I lay with my cheek pressed to his firm chest.

"Very ready," I grinned.

"I got you something," he surprised me by saying. I eyed the beautiful diamond ring he'd slipped on to my finger the same evening he'd proposed and wondered what else he could possibly have to give me. He gently moved me so he could sit up, pulling what looked like a jewelry box out from his bedside drawer.

"What's this?" I asked, sitting up cross-legged on the bed.

"Open it." He shrugged, his intense expression countering the casual movement.

I opened the box and sucked in a gasp. Inside, sat a beautiful silver necklace, almost identical to the one my grandmother had given me. The one I'd been forced to leave behind. I was floored that he'd remembered.

I simply stared at it for a few beats feeling warm tears slide down my face.

"Hey, what's this?" he asked, quietly swiping my tears away. "It wasn't supposed to make you sad."

"It doesn't," I assured him hoarsely, my eyes lifting to meet his. "It's just so beautiful and so incredibly thoughtful. I'm just so…" I searched for the right word settling on the one that eclipsed everything I felt. "Happy." I smiled through tears. "Thank you." I leaned in to kiss him deeply.

"You're welcome, darlin'. Is it close?" he asked with a wrinkled brow and I knew he meant the likeness.

"Very," I nodded, unclasping the necklace and putting it around my neck. He moved my hair over to my shoulder and fastened it securely in place around my neck.

It was close to my heart where, like Axel himself, I planned to keep it for the rest of my days.

Chapter Seventeen

The small part of me that had been concerned Ryker wouldn't take his officiant duties seriously, needn't have worried. From the moment I walked down the aisle with Sal, watching Axel's eyes grow bright and his chest heave with a shuddering breath, Ry had led us through the ceremony with a type of assured calm I hadn't seen in him before.

I clasped the large hands of my gorgeous husband-to-be and let Ryker's soothing voice wash over me. Holding Maddox for part of our vows, we promised to devote our lives to each other, to be the family we'd never had. With tears obscuring my vision, I put my gold ring on his finger where it would stay forever.

"I love you, Sophie," he said with a fierce growl after Ry had pronounced us husband and wife. He kissed me with a passion not entirely appropriate given the fact that we had an audience. I didn't give a damn and gave as good as I got. He pressed his forehead to mine, our breathing labored and a different kind of warmth spread across my skin.

"I love you, too," I smiled, rising on my tiptoes to kiss him again.

From there, it was all a blur of loud music, good food and rowdy revelry. The Knights knew how to party and I was happy to be swept up into the chaos. Everyone from the club was there and even a few Sinners too.

Kat had volunteered to watch Maddox and Scarlet seemed to be unofficially helping quite a bit with Mason.

In one of the few relatively quiet moments of the evening, I found a seat next to Jill who sat alone, admiring the view out on the deck. "Okay?" I asked, taking the seat at her side.

"Wonderful," she smiled. "You are gorgeous." She stroked a finger over the tulle of my skirt.

"Thanks. How long do you plan to stay?" I wanted to know, watching Axel as he stood laughing inside with Cole.

"I may not leave," she muttered as my head whipped around to face her.

"What? What's going on, Jill?" I asked as forcefully as I dared.

She shrugged, her posture too deliberate, too casual for my liking.

"Jill?" I pressed.

"I left Tim."

The silence weighed heavily between us as I tried desperately not to react too strongly to her words.

"How can I help?" I asked instead.

"You're already doing it. All this," she gestured to the festivity inside "it's a wonderful distraction," she sighed wistfully.

"Stay as long as you'd like." I reached over to grasp her hand in mine. "I love having you here," I told her truthfully.

"Thanks, Soph," she murmured and I could tell the

subject was nearing a close. I'd press for more details later. This wasn't the time.

Scar poked her head out then, holding Mason. "I think he's hungry. Should I feed him?" she asked.

Jill shook her head. "I'll do it, thanks." She smiled, rising to take her son. "Thank you for watching him."

"Sure," Scarlet smiled, winking at me before walking back inside to Cole.

I followed suit in search of my new husband.

It was nearing morning by the time we wound things down. Despite the evening's festivities and the hour, sleep was far from either of our minds.

"Ahhhhhh!" my cry was loud and piercing as Axel claimed me, driving so deep, it was as though he sought to pierce my soul.

His chuckle was low and satisfied as he lowered his lips to my ear. "Good thing we don't have any house guests," he rasped, his teeth finding purchase in the flesh of my neck.

Jill had taken Mason to stay at Kat's old apartment. The club had bought the place, rightfully thinking they'd need it again. It had been a safe haven for many visitors, myself included.

His lips moved to my breasts, sucking greedily as I raked my fingernails down his broad back.

"You're mine," he growled. "Mine to love, to protect, to fuck," he groaned as his thrusts became more rapid.

"Yes," I cried out at his words and from the onset of my orgasm.

"Baby," he groaned, his tone nearly reverent as he found his own release.

I wrapped my limbs around him, pulling him closer

and relishing the feel of our sweat – of our heartbeats intermingling with a resounding tempo.

He rolled us so that we were side by side with my thigh thrown over his hip. "This looks good," I sighed, my fingers tracing the outline of his wedding band.

"Yeah," he agreed as he nuzzled my throat.

"Again?" I giggled.

"Again," he growled.

When Mad woke us up the next morning, it felt like we'd just fallen asleep. We'd had many offers from friends to keep him overnight but we wanted him with us.

We chose to spend a quiet day as a family. Though it was nothing new for us to be together, there was something incredibly special to cement our vows, just the three of us.

We took lunch to the nursing home and celebrated with Sybil. We'd wanted to break her out of the home for a day to attend the ceremony but the nurses had recommended against it. The commotion and the new faces could have easily set her off. Instead, we had a quiet little celebration with sandwiches and sparkling apple cider. It was perfect.

I hadn't asked if we'd be seeing his mother. I knew what the answer was. On occasion, he still got a call – and he always went without question. The difference was that now when he got home, he didn't shut down, he talked. About how pissed off he was with her. About her lost opportunity with Maddox; I knew that hurt him the most. He was willing to share but he didn't want her to be part of our lives and I understood that, respected it.

Ry had at least convinced Ax to take him with him most of the time. He wanted to share the burden. Axel had protected him his whole life; he wanted to give some of that back.

It did nothing to cure their mother's addictions, but for two brothers dealing with a mother that had abandoned them for the bottle, it helped.

That evening as the three of us ate dinner, laughing as Maddox got more mashed potatoes in his hair than his mouth, I beamed with contentment. I couldn't think of a better way to celebrate. Just us. Just love.

It was a good thing we had that time considering all hell was about to break loose.

Chapter Eighteen

Early the next morning I felt Axel sit up abruptly. He vaulted out of bed before I could even form a question. When he slipped back into the room, I sat up, startled. "Wha—" I started to ask as he drew a finger to his lips to silence me.

Crap, that wasn't good.

The gun I now noticed in his hand also wasn't good.

"Get dressed, darlin'," he whispered.

"What's happening?" I whispered back.

"We've got company."

I felt my eyes widen to saucers as I scrambled out of bed, grabbing my clothes. His knowing eyes watched my frantic movements, a beacon of calm despite the circumstances.

"What kind of company?" I asked as I threw on my jeans and tank top, hopping around the room as I struggled into my boots. "Where's Maddox?"

"He's fine. It's okay. Calm down," he instructed, turning back to face me. "There's a car parked just off the road. Ry spotted it. We're gonna be cautious and head to the club," he explained.

"Right." I jerked my head in a nod and took a shaky breath in.

He crossed the room, putting his large hands on my shoulders and stooped to my eye level. "Babe, calm, okay? I've got you."

I met his eyes and relaxed a fraction. "Okay," I breathed. I threw on a sweater and my purse over my shoulder. "Ready," I added with a tilt of my chin.

I thought I saw a note of pride in his eyes at my resolve when he nodded and took my hand. "Grab Mad. We're gonna go out the garage, in my truck. Ry's gonna be right behind us."

"What's Ryker even doing here? It's so early," I thought to ask.

"I've had a man on the house every night," he answered as though that detail wasn't important to share. We'd be having that conversation later.

"Sorry, baby," I cooed to Maddox as I lifted him gently out of the crib. His little rosy cheeks were warm and soft as I swept my fingers over his face. He looked around, his beautiful eyes clouded with sleep as I carried him from the room.

Axel led us through the dimly lit house, the first hint of dawn barely making a dent through the darkness.

Ryker caught up with us in the living room, his expression taut as he and Axel flanked me. Both men wore shoulder holsters, guns at the ready and the whole situation was more than a little daunting considering I was still half-asleep.

Ax clipped Maddox into his car seat before drawing me around and hoisting me into the passenger side, pressing a chaste kiss to my lips before shutting my door.

I heard him exchange a few words with Ryker, though I couldn't make them out.

"Seatbelt," he instructed when he'd slid in the driver's seat. He looked over at me. "I'm gonna drive fast but I know what I'm doin'. Got it?"

"Got it," I nodded, my heart thumping painfully hard in my chest.

"Good," he muttered, hitting the garage door.

He wasn't kidding.

The second we could clear the door, he floored it, shooting us off into the rose-colored morning, kicking up gravel as we went. I heard the roar of a bike behind us and knew Ryker wasn't far behind.

I risked a glance in the passenger side mirror and shuddered at seeing a black town car giving chase.

"Don't worry about it," Axel muttered before I could comment.

He was in complete control. He didn't even appear stressed and I had to admit I was impressed. I'd never seen someone so calm under pressure.

I, on the other hand, was about to pee my pants.

His phone rang then and he answered with a barked, "Yeah?" He listened for a moment, his eyes glancing to the rearview every few moments. "Just one for now. At the speed I plan to drive? Ten minutes tops. Yeah, bud, see ya." He clicked off, shoving his phone into the console.

We got closer to town, hitting the main road, and Axel really picked up speed as I heard another bike's engine behind us.

"Tag," Axel explained calmly before I could ask.

When we arrived at the club, Axel and the guys pulled directly into the garage bay with Hank there to pull the large metal door shut before we'd even turned the engine off.

"Okay?" Axel turned to me to ask.

I managed a nod though my heart was still pounding. I climbed down from the large truck and wrapped my arms around myself protectively as Axel lifted Maddox out of his car seat.

Axel moved to stand beside me, taking my hand in his. The gesture nearly made me forget our current circumstances as my heart melted a bit. "Coffee?" he asked me quietly.

"Coffee," I agreed.

I was surprised to see so many people already there when we entered the main room. Cole, Mack and Ettie, Cal, and Wes and Connie were milling around when Axel and I walked in along with Hank and Tag.

"How you holding up?" Connie asked, approaching with a reassuring smile and a brief hug.

"Not a great way to wake up," I mumbled. "But I'm okay. Do we know who it is or how many there are?" I asked the room in general.

"Ry's out scouting," Wes replied, taking a sip of coffee, his dark gaze steady. Everyone seemed so relaxed, like this happened every day and the effect was contagious. I calmed down as well and went to grab a cup for Axel and me.

"Scar's with Gracie?" I asked Connie.

She nodded, sitting in Wes's lap.

I'd managed to eat something and had ingested enough coffee to fuel a jet when Ry swept into the club with a clenched jaw.

I immediately sat up straighter, watching as he walked directly to Cole and Axel, exchanging quiet words.

Axel looked over to me briefly, his face very intentionally

devoid of emotion, which I didn't take as a good sign.

"Oh, shit," I breathed quietly to no one in particular.

"We've got this covered," Wes' voice surprised me as he moved into view and sat next to me on the couch.

"I know you do," I agreed quietly, meaning it.

"He's been preparing for this eventuality – even without knowing the state of play,"

"And what eventuality would that be?" I asked cautiously.

"Ax can talk to you about it," he waved his hand dismissively before his expression grew serious. "You're covered, Soph, by all of us."

"Thanks, Wes," I nodded.

"Sophie!" I heard Axel's deep voice call from the office. "Come here a second!"

I rose to stand with an exasperated huff at his bossy bellow.

"Hey, sis, don't let him give you any shit," Wes grinned, lightening the mood.

"Right," I muttered, tossing a grin back at him as I handed Mad off to Connie.

How anyone thought I could contain a man like Axel was beyond me. But I was more than willing to give it a shot.

I found Axel, Cole and Mack all huddled around Cal's desk as I leaned on the doorway, eyeing them all with apprehension. "Okay, which one of you is going to tell me what the hell is going on?" I demanded.

They all looked up at me, surprise on their faces at my tone.

Then Axel grinned, clearly liking my sass. "That would be me," he replied, crooking a finger in my direction.

"Good luck, dude," Mack muttered as he and Cole exited the room with alarming speed.

"Why do you need luck?" I asked with a narrowed gaze.

"Come here, babe," he beckoned, gesturing to the couch as he moved to sit down.

I huffed, my lack of sleep and caffeine jitters getting the best of me.

"What is it?" he pressed.

I threw up my hands. "I'm tired and overwhelmed. I'm just trying to hang the hell on," I tried to explain.

He surprised me then by grabbing my hand and pressing it to his firm chest. "Then hang on to me," he commanded.

I looked down at where his hand covered mine against his firm chest. Then I looked into his grey eyes so steady and sincere. "Okay," I rasped.

He blew out a breath. "Your father has goons all over this fuckin' town, honey," he shared.

I felt my eyes widen. "What? Why?" I demanded.

He shook his head. "The man isn't right in the head, babe. Who knows what he's thinking. He might want proof you're married. He might be making a grab for you. Or it could just be an intimidation tactic." He snorted at the last part. "Whatever the reason, we need to take care of this shit. That includes getting rid of the men he's sent and dealing with your father.

"I don't imagine you want me to put him in the ground," he paused, waiting as I promptly shook my head. "Right. Well, then my next best option is to put him in jail."

"How are you going to do that?" I asked, feeling

numbness seep through my veins. Despite everything that happened, moments like this still took on a surreal quality that I had trouble grasping.

"Leverage," he shrugged. "Listen," he grasped my upper arms gently for emphasis as his gaze held mine. "Me and the club well, we've done a lot of work to prepare for this eventuality. But at the end of the day, shit like this – it has a way of goin' a couple of different directions. I don't want to tell you the plan and have you panic when it doesn't play out the way I expected. You okay with trusting me on this one?"

I loved that he knew me well enough and respected the fact that I wanted to know what was happening. I also knew he was right.

"Yeah, babe," I leaned toward his body, pressing my forehead to his. "I trust you."

"I know he's your father," his deep voice continued, "but darlin', if he does anything to threaten you or Maddox I can't promise—"

"I understand," I cut him off. "He's my father but you and Maddox are my family," I added, stroking my fingers through his unruly hair.

"There's a whole room of people out there who are your family, too," he told me.

Tears pricked the back of my eyes as I nodded, biting my lip against the emotion burning through me.

"I would take you away from this shit but this is the safest place for you and Maddox. So you'll stay here until this is over."

"How long will that be?"

His answer was simple, his tone biting. "Soon."

******

"I'm kinda bored," Jill stage whispered.

"I'm suuuuper bored," Connie groaned.

"You guys are so dramatic." Scarlet rolled her eyes. "It's been like three hours. We hang out here longer than that all the time."

All the girls had been brought in, Jill included, for protection.

"At least we can normally go outside," Ettie put in, flipping through one of the magazines Scarlet had brought.

"Sorry," I mumbled, feeling responsible for their predicament.

"Oh, shit, Soph, we're assholes. Sorry," Connie rushed to apologize.

I shrugged. "It's my fault. I brought all this down on you." I looked off to the side.

"Uh, no," Jill shook her head emphatically. "Your asshole parents did that."

"Soph, seriously. If we played the blame game, I'd be front and center for the shit my past caused," Scarlet spoke up. "I learned a long time ago to let that shit go. Axel would much rather have you in his life and deal with this than the alternative. So would all of us."

"Thanks," I offered a small smile, accepting her one-armed hug.

"Where's the chocolate?" Kat demanded from one of the couches where she was currently sprawled, swollen feet resting. The guys had disappeared down the hall a while ago, but that didn't stop Sal from coming out periodically to make sure she was resting.

"Here," I smiled, handing her a piece from our stash. The magazines and chocolate should get us through at least another hour. After that, we would need to get creative.

At least the kids were entertained. Mason, Maddox, and Gracie were playing together sweetly as we looked on. Well, more like Mason and Maddox were watching Gracie toddle around, but nevertheless, they seemed content.

"Axel wants another," I confided. It had come up a few times, even in the last few days. Once all this drama died down, I was willing to consider it.

"Cole's getting another," Scarlet said, her eyes bright.

"What!" Kat shrieked.

"Keep your voice down," Scarlet laughed. "And for God's sake, don't get up. We don't need the pregnancy police back out here."

"How far along are you?" Jill asked.

"About ten weeks, still early," Scar answered, looking over at Gracie with a serene smile.

"Congratulations," I offered, so happy for her.

"Thanks," she grinned.

I looked at the women around me, thrilled our extended family was about to get just a little bit bigger.

"Still wanting to stay?" I asked Jill quietly a little while later. The kids were all down for a nap in the back rooms along with Kat and Scarlet. Jill and I sat side by side on one of the couches, browsing through magazines we'd already read ten times.

"Yeah," she shrugged. "I like it here. And you're here," she poked me playfully.

"I'm glad," I smiled.

"I need to start working. You all have been far too generous already," she sighed.

"Take your time," I soothed. "There's no rush."

"We'll see," she answered evasively.

I was nearly nodding off myself on the couch when a

commotion woke me up. I had to blink a few times when I saw Axel and Wes hauling Benjamin McKenzie across the room. I shook my head as though to clear it.

Nope, I wasn't seeing things. That was definitely Benjamin, the son of a New York senator being hauled across the Knights' club floor.

Axel met my wide gaze and shocked me by tilting his head toward the back rooms with a cocked brow. He was asking if I wanted to follow or turn a blind eye.

I got up and followed, ignoring his exasperated sigh.

"What the fuck, man!" Benjamin protested as Axel hauled him into a room toward the back of the club. I followed tentatively, feeling like I was invading a space I didn't belong in. Cole and Sal both leaned against the far wall, their arms crossed. Mack, Hank and Ryker all stood to my left watching Benjamin with pure hostility. I'd never seen this part of the club. It was a simple room with no furniture save for one piece. One chair sat in the middle of the room. Despite its simplicity, its placement invited a certain sinister-like quality. I swallowed audibly and I wasn't even the one who was going to have to sit in it.

"Sit the fuck down," Axel ordered, shoving Benjamin into it.

"What the hell? Do you have any idea who my father is?" he sputtered, trying to straighten his white polo. His eyes darted around the room, growing wider by the moment. When they fell on me, he recoiled with shock, – his expression confused.

"Sophie? What the hell are you doing here? Did these fucks kidnap you, too?"

Axel smacked the back of his head with a resounding whack that sent his head snapping forward. "She's my wife."

"Wife?" Benjamin looked thoroughly confused, rubbing at the back of his head.

"Yeah, so I'd say those plans of yours are pretty much to shit now," Axel muttered, walking slow circles around Benjamin's chair. He was the epitome of menace as his slow, calculated steps continued.

He was in his element and I suddenly understood why he'd been so upset when he'd had to let the guys handle things before. He exuded pure menace with a cool confidence I was thoroughly impressed by. I'd always known Axel could handle himself, but seeing him like this, I understood it on a different level.

Ben's gaze turned to me. "Your father is going to be so pissed," he shook his head. "This was never *my* plan."

"I figured, given how we got you here," Axel returned.

"Yeah, about that," Benjamin stammered, his eyes wide as they shot around the room.

"What? You don't want dear old Dad to know you have a thing for hookers?" Sal snorted. "That you were looking to score enough blow to turn the state white?"

Despite myself, I nearly laughed. This was all just too freaking ironic.

"You should really think about diversifying. You're too fucking predictable," Mack put in, cracking his knuckles. "Coming all the way to Las Vegas for some pussy and blow." He shook his head in mock admonishment. "I mean, don't get me wrong, I'm so glad our girl, Tracy, was hot enough to reel you in, but seriously, dude, don't they have decent pussy in New York?"

I took it all in, realizing how much effort they'd put in to get Benjamin here. Even using one of the club chicks as part of the ruse. I was seriously impressed. I wondered what the plan from here was.

"What do you want?" Benjamin glared.

"I want you to deliver the message that Sophie's already spoken for," Axel began, stopping his slow circle to stand in front of the chair. "I want you to make it fucking clear that any future marriage is off the table. And," he continued, pulling Benjamin's head back so he was forced to glare up into Axel's face, "I want all the fucking knowledge you have on her father. Anything less and all your conversations with Tracy and all the other shit we dug up on you gets spread far and wide," he threatened, before letting go of his hair with such force that his head snapped forced. Axel stepped back with his arms crossed over his broad chest and waited.

"You think I know shit about her father?" Benjamin protested.

"I know you do," Axel bit out.

"If you know so much, then what do you even need me for?" he demanded.

"Proof," Axel shrugged.

Benjamin hesitated, sweat beading along his brow as he licked his lips nervously and shook his head. "I don't know anything.".

"Babe," Axel spoke to me, his eyes moving to find mine. I knew what he was saying without needing the words. This was the part where things could get ugly. Again, he gave me the choice.

I nodded in understanding, slipping from the room.

I knew Axel operated outside of the confines of the law and he did that a lot. I also knew he was the best husband and father I could have ever dreamed of. That was what mattered to me.

******

"It's not enough, man," I heard Cole mutter as I was getting Maddox up from his nap a little while later. They probably thought I was still in the main room with the girls, far from earshot. "It's a lot more than we had, but not enough."

"I know," I heard Axel growl with frustration.

"What's next?" Mack asked.

"Holy shit," I heard Sal's intake of breath and my body went rigid at his tone. "You're not going to fucking believe who I see on the video feed standing out front."

Chapter Nineteen

M y mother stood in the middle of the main room in her crisp designer outfit looking like a fish out of water. Not a hair was out of place, not a wrinkle to be found, yet her eyes gave away her frazzled state.

"Sophie," her voice rang out through the large room as I emerged, holding Maddox in my arms.

I felt Axel's warmth at my back, providing unspoken support and comfort as I moved deeper into the room.

"What are you doing here?" I asked, noting the quiet audience we had as the girls looked on with wide eyes and the men stood scattered throughout the room, watching our exchange.

Her hand flew over her mouth as it visibly shook. "Is that…?" Her voice was a ragged whisper as she looked at Maddox.

"My son. Our son," I amended with a nod, looking up at Axel.

"Oh, God," she breathed.

Mad squealed, reaching his arms up for his daddy. Axel took him in his arms, moving to stand to my right as Sal took my left.

"Sal," her voice was a murmur as she took us both in.

"What are you doing here?" his voice was cold and unyielding. For every bit of misguided attention she'd forced on me as a child, the only thing she'd offered Sal was indifference.

Sal's father was a Spanish man from humble roots. Though I think my mother had loved him, she removed him from her life in search of pedigree and prestige.

My father had fit the bill to a T. I couldn't fathom choosing money over love.

"I want to help," she replied, effectively shocking the hell out of me.

"Come again?" Sal demanded.

She glanced around, clearly uncomfortable by the amount of eyes on her. "Can we talk, in private?"

I looked to Axel and then to Sal, letting them make the decision. After a brief moment of hesitation, Axel nodded.

"Take Mad," he instructed Ryker, carefully handing our son to his uncle. He grasped my hand, his touch warm and firm as he led us back to Cal's office.

Axel and Sal leaned against the desk as my mother took a seat. I couldn't remain that still and stood, leaning against the wall pensively.

"Talk," Sal ordered brusquely and despite myself, I winced at his tone.

"I know I've made a lot of mistakes, with both of you," she began. "Despite what you may think, I love you both very much." She swallowed as I sucked in a surprised breath. I could remember only one other occasion where she'd said she loved me in my entire life. "I've had a lot of time to reflect this last year. I've lost both of you and I want to try to make things right." She twisted her hands in her lap, a nervous gesture I'd never seen in her before. She was always so put together, so impenetrable.

"Your father…" She shook her head, looking at me. "His sanity has…well, he's changed," she said primly, trying to hold on to her pride while delivering what I was sure she considered shameful news. "He's obsessed with bringing you home. I'm worried he's going to do something brash. Well, more brash," she amended.

"You know he has men here in Hawthorne scouting?" Axel cut in.

She winced. "I didn't know for sure. But I've caught wind of some of his conversations. I knew he might be planning something."

"He belongs in the fucking nut house," Sal muttered.

"You might be right," she allowed. "I left him." She shared the shocking news with quiet dignity. "I gathered what I could. I think it will help," she offered, pulling a large file out of her purse and handing it over to Sal.

Sal reviewed the file, his brows lifting before he handed it over to Axel. "It will," Sal nodded.

My shoulders sagged with relief, ready to be done with this insanity.

"Do you think after all this is over – if I came back to town, that we could talk?" she asked cautiously, her gaze snapping from mine to Sal's.

A heavy silence followed her words as Sal remained motionless with his arms crossed and gaze to his boots. I could understand his reaction but as for me well, I wanted to believe that redemption was possible.

"Maybe," I nodded.

"Maybe," she swallowed, accepting the words before rising and straightening her blouse. "He's beautiful," she told me and I knew she meant Maddox.

"Thank you." I nodded, moving toward Axel as he lifted his arm to pull me into his body.

She gathered her things and left the room without another word.

The sob that escaped me was unexpected and sudden. I curled into Axel's big body as his arms came up around me holding me tightly.

"I'll go see her out," Sal offered, leaving us a few moments together.

"Baby." Axel's sigh was sympathetic as he held me tighter still.

"I don't know why I'm crying!" I sputtered. "She was always so mean to me but I guess I miss her, which is so screwed up."

He squeezed me tighter. "She's your mom." He knew firsthand how deep that love ran and how confusing it could be.

"Yeah," I agreed hoarsely.

"For what it's worth, she just gave us the rest of the information we need."

"Really?" I pulled back, looking up at him as he wiped my tears away.

"Yeah, babe. We're gonna be able to end this. Soon."

I blew out a relieved breath. "Good."

*****

With the information my mother had provided handed off to the police, an arrest warrant had been issued for my father. It was a rare show of partnership between the Knights and the local PD. Not something, Axel assured me, I was likely to see again.

I didn't know the details of the charges and, at the moment, didn't care. I assumed Axel would tell me what I needed to know. I was focused on keeping Maddox content and hoping we'd be in our own beds that night.

A group of the guys went out scouting and came back confirming that his cronies had left town. Too many cops, too much heat for them to stick around. Plus, I'd guess with their boss about to be locked up, there wasn't much reason for them to stick around. There'd be nobody to pay them.

It was late by the time the guys agreed it was safe enough for all of us to disperse.

Ryker had decreed he'd be staying with us for the night, wanting Axel to have him at his back. It'd been a long day and all I wanted was to get home.

Home.

"What's on your mind?" Axel asked, his head cocked toward me as we drove up the mountain with Ryker's bike rumbling behind us.

There was so much going through my mind just then, but mostly, I was thinking about how all of this was nearly behind us and together, we could just look forward.

"I was thinking about the house," I answered him.

His brow lifted and I could tell that wasn't the answer he'd been expecting.

"I was thinking it's time we made some changes, work on Mad's room," I explained.

"Guess I had to put a ring on your finger for you to come to that conclusion, finally," he goaded me with a chuckle.

"Whatever," I huffed as he reached over and tickled my side.

"Hey!" I protested through laughter as Mad squealed from the backseat.

"Your mama's ticklish," Axel told him, his deep chuckle reverberating through the small space as I continued to squeal.

"Okay, okay," I held up my hands in surrender as he grabbed one and placed it in his lap.

"You did good today," he told me quietly.

I sighed. "Thanks."

"The shit with your dad, are you okay with it?"

"I don't know that I'll ever be okay with it necessarily." I bit my lip and looked out the window as the dark landscape slid by. "But I understand why it has to be this way. It's better than a lot of the alternatives. Do you think they'll catch him soon?"

He squeezed my hand. "Yeah."

"Good," I sighed, suddenly weary. "I'm ready to be done with this."

"I know, darlin'."

"What did he do?" I asked seriously.

Ax glanced over to me, his expression sympathetic, which didn't bode well. "You sure?"

I knew he wanted to protect me from this, but I needed to know.

"Yeah," I nodded.

"He's been into some serious shit for a while," he began as I braced myself for what was to come. "Seems like he's got a pretty serious gambling problem."

"My father?" I demanded incredulously. I would never have guessed.

"Yep, he's broke...as in bankrupt. That's why he was after your money. One thing we did learn from Benjamin

198

was that there was a substantial financial gain for your father if you married him. It had the potential to rebuild his completely fucked career also."

"So what was his plan? To sell me off?" I screeched.

He put a hand on my thigh and squeezed in reassurance. "Not sure," he admitted.

"Do you think my mother knows?"

"The information she gave us was pretty damning so I'd guess whatever she didn't know before she does now. I also don't think she had any part in trying to steal from your trust fund. She actually delivered proof that he'd fraudulently tried to access your money."

I felt an unexpected wave of sympathy for my mother. Despite everything, I didn't want her to lose everything she had. She'd already lost her family.

"One thing I'll say for your mother, babe. She may be a bitch but the lady is smart. I'm sure she can take care of herself," he assured me, picking up on my line of thinking.

"I hope so," I bit my lip. I thought about everything he just shared, trying to make sense of an insane situation. "So basically, his whole plan centered around me. He lost everything by being a jackass and thought he could marry me off to some rich senator's son and somehow reclaim power and money."

"Pretty much."

"What an ass." I shook my head in disgust.

"Yeah, well, your mother obviously has the brains in that relationship. He didn't cover his tracks very well. The money was an easy trail to follow – Sal and I have been on that for weeks."

My anger flared, sudden and intense. "Why didn't you say anything?" I hissed, not wanting to yell and scare

Maddox.

He turned to face me briefly before his eyes returned to the dark road ahead. "I wanted to have proof before I had to deliver more bad news," he answered with gruff sincerity. "We all know your father's a grade A bastard, but all this," he shook his head. "It's worse than I thought it would be."

That pacified me some though I still wished he would have told me.

"What's his connection with the Black Riders?" I wanted to know. "I don't get how he even knew how to contact Aron, or Jeb for that matter. "

Axel jaw clenched. "It's fucked up," he admitted. "And we still don't know everything, including who was feeding him information about our club. He often came to Vegas to gamble. The Black Riders run a lot of that territory. I don't know how it started, but somewhere along the way, he invested in several of their businesses. He got in way over his head," Axel sighed in exasperation. "You don't live long with an outstanding debt with a club like theirs," he said darkly. "My guess is, Aron got wind that the Black Riders were owed a pay day and struck out on his own working with Jeb to get inside information. They didn't realize your dad was broke. They got greedy."

"What's going to happen with the Black Riders now?" I wanted to know.

"Cal wants to find out how much their prez knows," he explained. "If it was just a debt they were owed, that's one thing. But, if he had anything to do with breaking into your place or your kidnapping, that's another. For now, we're still thinking Aron and Jeb were acting alone." When he saw my worried expression, his deep voice rumbled,

"Don't worry, baby,"

Easier said than done, but I nodded rather than argue.

"Thank you," I murmured, turning to watch his handsome profile as he watched the road intently.

He turned to look at me briefly, his eyes soft. "For what?"

"Where do I start?" I smiled tenderly, reaching over to stroke his bearded jaw. I decided to settle on the easiest answer. "For everything."

He lifted my hand to kiss my knuckles. "Always, baby."

"Always," I agreed.

Despite everything, I felt like the luckiest girl in the whole world.

Chapter Twenty

"Did you, uh, cook the eggs?" Ry asked cautiously the next morning. I'd wanted to cook breakfast for the guys but my culinary skills still required some practice evidently.

"Yeah, why?" I asked, leaning over to look at my handiwork on their plates. Maddox babbled in my arms and I moved him to my other hip. He was getting so big.

The eggs did look slightly runny, but last time I'd overcooked them.

Dammit.

Axel shot him a glare but Ryker threw up his hands in reply. "Dude, I know she's your wife and I love her like a sister, but that doesn't mean I'm going to let her poison me!"

I rolled my eyes, shoving a box of cereal at him and tried not to take it personally when Axel was the first to reach for it.

He pulled me over so I stood between his muscular thighs with Maddox cradled in my arms. "You wanna start on Mad's room today?" His eyes burned with an intensity that was now familiar but no less butterfly-inducing.

"Yeah," I agreed softly.

He tweaked the rings on my left hand and grinned. "That's good, babe. I think I'll even have another set of hands with this knucklehead." He hooked a thumb in Ry's direction.

"Great," Ry muttered as he shoved a huge bite of cereal into his mouth.

As it turned out, we had more help than we needed. Sal and Cole stopped by to check on things and stayed to help dismantle the office. Scarlet and Connie offered to stay with Mad and Gracie while Kat and I went into town to buy some new things for the nursery with Mack and Wes in tow.

The image of Wes and Mack folding their big bodies into the rocking chairs at the front of the children's store while we shopped would be permanently burned into my mind. Perfect material for whenever I'd need a quick laugh – for the next twenty years.

"What are you guys going to do for Thanksgiving?" Kat asked as we sifted through racks of baby clothes. We'd picked out the furniture for the room relatively quickly and had soon grown distracted with the tiny clothing for Kat's little one.

I grimaced. "Well, if I wanted to punish Ax, I could cook." I hadn't given the holiday much thought despite it being just a few weeks away.

She laughed. "Well, I think Scar is planning to host. You guys should come. Invite Jill."

"I'll talk to her," I nodded.

"I'll make sure Cal is coming." She winked as though I was in on the secret.

My brows knit with confusion. "Why would you do that?"

She looked at me with wide eyes. "He's sweet on her," she replied as though I were daft.

"I didn't notice," I admitted, embarrassed at how little attention I'd obviously been paying my best friend. Clearly, I needed to rectify that. "She's going through some stuff; I don't know if…" I trailed off.

"He knows," she interjected with assurance.

How?

"I've been a terrible friend," I shook my head with a grimace.

"You've been through some serious shit, girl. Cut yourself some slack," Kat admonished, linking her arm through mine and towing me toward the register.

"Finally," Wes muttered.

"Hey, this'll be you someday," Kat retorted, gesturing to all the baby clothes she cradled.

He had a moment of wide-eyed acknowledgement. "Fuck me," he muttered, shaking his head.

"Well, that won't bring a baby around anytime soon," Kat replied with a wink in my direction.

"Christ, you chicks love to bust my fucking balls," he retorted as I fought my struggle and let the laugh I'd been fighting burst out.

Mack's deep-throated chuckle filled the space as he got a good laugh at Wes' expense.

By the time we got home, I was impressed with how much work they'd done. The guys had all cleared out except for Ryker. The office was completely empty and Axel was painting it a beautiful grey-blue.

"Get what you needed?" he asked when he saw me standing in the doorway.

"Yeah," I smiled. "Looks good in here. The delivery

folks will be bringing everything up shortly. It was all in stock."

"Good," he nodded, looking thoughtfully at the wall. "You know, I never thought to ask if you wanted to stay here. This was my place that I rebuilt with Ry. It has meaning to me but…" he trailed off.

I moved into the room, wrapping arms around him from behind. "This is the first real home I've ever known. I love it," I assured him.

"I'm glad," he nodded, turning in my arms and laying his lips over mine.

"I wouldn't mind doing some updating though?" I mentioned hesitantly against his lips.

He chuckled. "Yeah, babe, we can do that. We'll have to expand someday, too," he winked, smacking my ass as I headed back out of the room.

"Right, for that football team you want to have." I rolled my eyes with a smile.

"Damn straight," he nodded.

The next few days felt like a tense waiting game. There was still no news on my father – the authorities were still looking for him. Axel was still on high alert with eyes on the house.

We finished the nursery and moved on to the master. The space that had always felt like home became something more. It became an oasis that I had put my own mark on. Putting Mad to bed every night in his beautiful room gave me a sense of peace I hadn't realized I'd been missing.

We kept up my driving lessons. I convinced Axel to let me practice on something smaller and we'd borrowed Connie's car a few times. I was much more confident than the first time I'd gotten behind the wheel.

If I could only learn not to burn everything I tried to cook, I'd be in pretty good shape.

Axel liked to tease me that miracles didn't happen overnight.

After many failed attempts, I ended up with something close enough to resembling pumpkin pie to bring to Thanksgiving dinner. It certainly wouldn't win any contests but at least it wouldn't kill anybody, hopefully.

Cole and Scarlet's house was packed with club members and their families as the smell of the holiday permeated the air.

"Here," I handed Scar my pie with a grimace. "It's the thought that counts, right?"

"Right," she nodded with a laugh, wrapping me in a one-armed hug.

The meal was delicious, the mood raucous and light in a way it hadn't been in several days. I watched Cal lean over and talk to Jill from my place across the table. Every time he spoke to her, which was often, her face flushed. She seemed hesitant to engage him, but there was something going on there.

"You're staring," Axel reprimanded me with a quiet chuckle.

"Fine," I grumbled, looking away from my source of curiosity and locking eyes with my husband. His beautiful eyes gleamed back at me. "I like staring at you better," I smiled.

"You better," he growled good-naturedly, grasping my thigh underneath the table.

"So how long are you in town for, Jill?" Connie asked when there was a general lull in the boisterous conversation.

Jill looked like a deer in headlights for a moment as the

silence weighed heavily on the table.

Connie's big blue eyes darted around nervously. "Sorry, was I not supposed to ask that?" she asked in the genuine and straightforward way that was pure Connie.

"No, it's fine," Jill rushed to assure her. "I'm just not sure."

"I heard there's an opening at the hospital," Scarlet put in. Scar had been in nursing school since I'd known her, but with a toddler and baby on the way, her progress had stalled some.

"Oh?" Jill asked. "Well, I have a lot to sort out." She shifted nervously in her seat and I waded in to her rescue.

"Jill's a hot commodity." I winked. "Where's Ry?" I asked, deliberately changing the subject.

I saw Jill literally deflate with relief when the focus wasn't on her anymore.

"Wrapped up in something," Wes snickered.

"Man whore," Ettie shook her head with a giggle.

"On Thanksgiving? Really?" I demanded. As much as Ry could be annoying at times, I missed him. I was mildly affronted that he'd picked a random bimbo over his family.

"Pumpkin pie's good but not nearly as good as pussy," Wes chortled as Connie smacked him; I turned to smother a laugh in Axel's shoulder.

It was after pie and to the point where I was stuffed to the gills when I finally had Jill alone for a minute. Rather than try to wrap her up in a conversation when we only had a spare moment, I tried to coax her up to our place for the night.

"I don't know, Soph," she fretted. "I don't want to put you out and I don't have any of Mason's overnight stuff."

"Okay, how about tomorrow then? Or I could come to

you?" I offered. I missed my friend and wanted to spend time together like we used to. We had a lot of catching up to do.

Axel came to stand alongside me, and Maddox immediately reached out of my arms for his daddy. "What's up?" Axel asked, picking our boy up and delivering a quick nuzzle into his neck.

"Jill and I were trying to sort out a sleepover," I informed him. "I was thinking I could stay with her tomorrow night.".

Axel turned to Jill. "I'll pick you up, bring you to our place."

"Babe," I sighed, exasperated.

"Got no problem with girls' night," he shook his head. "But I want you under our roof."

"That's fine," Jill assured him, shooting me a look to relax.

"Fine," I grumbled. "How are you getting home?"

"Uh, Cal has Mason's car seat in his truck. I guess he's taking me home," she replied nervously.

"Okay, well, you're in good hands then," I answered her softly, reaching out to squeeze her hand.

"Yeah," she bit her lip, not meeting my eye.

Weird. I didn't know this side of Jill. The woman I knew was bold and unafraid to speak her mind.

"Let's go," Axel said a short while later. His demeanor had been surly after dinner and I couldn't understand why. We'd had a great night.

"Sure," I agreed, eyeing him warily.

We said our goodbyes and headed out into the chilly evening. "Will we get snow soon you think, up at the house?" I wondered aloud as he fired up the engine and pointed us toward home.

"Possibly," he shrugged.

"I hope it snows for Christmas." I grinned at the thought of a warm fire and cozy day. Just for us. "Can we get our tree soon?"

"Sure," he shrugged pensively.

I was getting a lot of shrugs and not many words out of him. Never a good sign.

"What's going on?" I demanded.

"Nothin'," he muttered.

"Okay," I replied, not in any hurry to have him spoil my upbeat mood.

We drove the majority of the ride home in silence with Maddox slumbering peacefully in his car seat.

It was a good deal colder up at our place and I rushed inside with Maddox wrapped in my arms.

The alarm beeped at me but I let Axel deal with it as I carried Mad to bed. He went down without a peep, tired from all the excitement of the evening.

I knew well enough by now to avoid Axel and whatever he was working through. Instead, I got ready for bed and slid under the warm covers, curling up with a baking book. I couldn't explain exactly why I was so hell bent on being able to cook. Maybe it was that my mother had never done it, that Axel's hadn't either. I certainly didn't feel like Axel expected it. It was more an expectation of myself; a huge hurdle of independence after a life beholden to others.

I'd studied the merits of coffee cake thoroughly by the time I turned out the light. Axel was pacing around the house, banging around as he seemed to do when he was in a dark mood.

As always, I had trouble sleeping until I felt Axel slide

into bed.

"Babe, what is it?" I asked, my voice hoarse with elusive sleep.

"Nothin'," he growled.

I slid up on an elbow peering over at him through the dim light. "Are you mad about something?"

His reply was cutting. "You seriously askin'?"

Then it dawned on me. "You're mad at me?" I replied in shock. "What the heck did I do?"

"Do you have any idea what the state of play is right now, Sophie? Any idea how much fucking danger there is? And you're offering to flit off with Jill like it's nothing! Wanting to spend the night in a not so great part of town without me!" he snarled.

It seemed I unleashed the beast with a simple question.

"It was just an idea, babe, Jesus," I snorted, exasperated with his attitude. I bit back the urge to give him a hard time for using the word "flit." Unfortunately, it didn't seem like a good time to tease him. Such a good morsel lost, damn.

"Do not blow me off about this," he growled.

"You didn't even want to talk about it until I forced it out of you!" I threw up my hands in frustration, sitting up in bed, sleep forgotten. "I understand it's dangerous out there. It's been dangerous for me since you met me," I exclaimed. "That doesn't mean I can't want simple things like a sleepover with my best friend without making her go out of her way," I tried to explain. "I know you wouldn't let me do something risky, nor would I go against something you were concerned about. As long as it's reasonable," I hastened to add. "All you have to do is explain why and we're good. You don't have to pace around the house all night like a goddamned lion," I said dryly.

"A lion?" he queried with a lifted brow.

I shrugged, my arms crossed.

He sighed, sitting with his back against the headboard, his chiseled abs on infuriatingly gorgeous display. "I admit I can be a possessive bastard," he nodded, running a hand over his beard. "But until your father is behind bars, until we know what's at play with the Riders, I need you close. Hell, I'll always want you close but especially now, Soph."

"That's all you have to say," I agreed, placing a hand on his stomach. "You don't have to go all grouch puss on a holiday because of it," I grumbled.

"Grouch puss? Babe, seriously," he griped at my choice of words.

"This was my first Thanksgiving with people I actually wanted to spend it with," I defended. "You going all alpha-male jackass allows for me to call you whatever I want," I told him haughtily.

He pulled me into his chest, kissing the top of my head. "I want to give you everything you want, holidays included. But your safety comes first. Please, babe," he practically pleaded.

"Yeah, honey," I agreed, kissing his chest.

"Wes had a point earlier," he trailed off as he rolled on top of me suddenly, making me shriek with laughter.

"And what was that?" I asked, smiling up into his face.

"Pussy's a hell of a lot better than any goddamned pumpkin pie," he grinned down at me looking positively gorgeous.

"Yeah?" I giggled with a lifted brow, relieved our fight had been short-lived.

"Yeah, though I'd say you'd taste damn good with some whipped cream."

Chapter Twenty-One

"I'm sorry I haven't been able to spend more time with you," I apologized the next night as Jill and I sat out on the back deck snuggled up in blankets. It was surprisingly cozy, especially with the heat lamp humming that I'd convinced Axel to get.

Both of us loved sitting outside, even in the cold, and frequently sat on the deck talking after Maddox had gone to bed.

"It's okay. You've had a lot going on." Jill reached over to squeeze my hand before taking a sip of her wine and gazing out into the forest beyond. Both boys were asleep and Axel made himself scarce, allowing us our time alone.

"So have you," I put in, trying not to press too hard but more than ready for her to share what had been going on. "Have you heard from him?" I asked quietly.

She grimaced. "Yeah. He's threatening legal action because I took Mason across state lines."

"What!" I exclaimed.

She nodded. "Yeah. The irony, right? He's barely seen Mason since he was born but now that we're not under his roof, he's fighting it tooth and nail. Even when he was in town, he never helped. He's never even seemed attached to

Mason," she swallowed audibly and I could tell how much that hurt her.

"What happened?" I asked.

"It wasn't one particular thing," she sighed. "We've been strangers for a long time. I could deal with the time away and raising Mason alone. Frankly, it was easier when he wasn't around. What I can't deal with is the husband I got when he did come home." She fought back a shudder.

"And what's that?" I pressed. It was clear she didn't like talking about this but I felt the need to understand so I could help in any way I could.

"Angry," she sighed. "So angry."

"At you?"

"At everything. I could deal with a lot. I'm even fairly sure he had something on the side."

"Oh, honey." I reached over, squeezing her hand.

"But he'd escalated lately, starting pushing me around. I won't have my son raised in that environment," she shook her head adamantly, moisture pooling in her eyes.

"He hit you?" I demanded, reading between the lines.

She paused, her fingers dancing nervously over the fringe of her blanket. "Yes."

"I'm so sorry," I breathed. "You never have to go back there," I added, reassuring myself as much as her. I'd known there were challenges in their marriage and that she wasn't happy. I had no idea it was that bad.

"Your wedding came at such a perfect time," she smiled through tears. "I needed to get out of town. Then everyone was so welcoming, even giving me a place to stay!" she marveled. "I kind of love it here. I'm just not sure how I'll support us if we stay," she fretted.

I hadn't wanted my or rather, our money to affect our

lives, but this was an opportunity for it to change someone else's. For the better. Someone I loved.

"Jill," I began, turning my body toward hers, choosing my words carefully. I knew if I approached this the wrong way, she'd balk. Hell, she'd probably do that anyway but I wanted to help her so vehemently that my heart was racing with the force of it. "Hear me out," I asked quietly as I organized my thoughts. "You know with all this stuff with my parents that I'm pretty damn heartbroken over it," I admitted. "It's a hard fact to grapple with that my father could sink as low as he has. The money from my trust fund, even though it's from my grandfather, well, I've struggled with it. I'm almost afraid to touch it – like it will somehow instantly propel me back to my old life," I laughed without humor at the absurdity of it all. Axel had asked me about it more than once. I knew I was irrational, but in some bizarre way, I felt like the money was tainted. Like if I touched it, the beautiful life we were building could disappear.

"But if I could do something great with it – something for you, well, it would help," I told her honestly.

Her eyes opened wide and she moved to shake her head.

"Please, Jill," I cut her off before she could speak. "You were there for me when no one else was. You taught me so much about being a mother when I was floundering and completely overwhelmed. You saved my life, Jill," I told her passionately. "I can't ever convey how pivotal you were in my life and Maddox's. And I know you don't want me to repay you, but let me return the favor in some small way. Let me do something with that money that'll help free you, something it never did for me."

"What about Axel? It's his money now too," she bit her lip and I tried not to grin that she was clearly considering it.

"I'll talk to him," I promised. "But he'll be fine with it," I assured her.

"What did you have in mind?" she asked quietly.

"You'll need a divorce lawyer," I began. "A good one. Let us help with that and childcare while you're getting back on your feet. I saw how excited you were about that job at the hospital," I pointed out. "You'll need someone to watch Mason if you want to go for that job. What is the arrangement with Kat's old place?"

"Cal won't let me pay for it," she grumbled. "I don't even know him!" she protested.

"If he made up his mind, good luck convincing him otherwise," I grinned. "It seems like he's taken a shine to you, hmm?" I hedged.

"I don't know, maybe," she shrugged, seeming confounded. "He's handsome – I mean, really freaking handsome. You'd have to be blind not to notice but I'm in a crazy head space right now. I can't deal with even thinking about anything romantic," she sighed. "If that's what he even wants," she hastened to add.

I looked at my beautiful friend and could only assume that was the case.

"For now, he's just been supportive from a distance. The whole club has been so awesome." She smiled fondly.

"Yeah, they really are," I agreed. "So does this all mean that you'll let us help you out?" I asked hopefully.

She sighed. "I feel beyond weird about it but my priority is getting sole custody of Mason. I can't afford a lawyer and clearly I need one. So yes, thank you," she agreed, seeming relieved.

I reached over and clasped her hand. "What are friends for?"

"Cal mentioned there being some sort of ceremony at the club tomorrow night," she said and I knew she was deliberately changing the subject.

"Ry's getting patched in," I grinned. I knew it meant the world to him and to Axel.

Her brows knitted together and I knew many aspects of the club were still foreign to her. "So he'll be officially part of the club?" she wondered.

"Yep," I nodded. "I don't know what the ceremony entails really," I admitted. "The guys are kind of mum on those details. But we're invited to the party afterwards. I probably won't be able to stay long with Maddox but you should come."

"Nah," she shook her head. "I'm sure it'll be rowdy, and with Mason, I wouldn't be able to stay long anyway. Why don't I watch Maddox for you so you can stay longer?" she offered.

I sighed, knowing already what Axel would say. "Thank you. Ordinarily, I'd take you up on that but I don't think Axel will go for it."

She nodded. "I get it."

It was late by the time we decided to turn in. Our bedroom was dark when I crawled under the covers snuggling up to Axel's warm body.

"Jesus, babe, you're freezing," his sleepy voice rasped as he wrapped his arms around me.

"We were sitting outside," I explained, nuzzling into his chest and breathing in his scent.

He grunted as I stuck my freezing nose against his skin.

"Have fun?"

I nodded. "It was good to catch up. We talked more about the situation with Tim. It's bad, babe. I had no idea. I feel so guilty," I shook my head.

"She obviously didn't want to share, darlin'. You both had your reasons for keeping secrets."

He was certainly right about that.

"True," I sighed. "I really want to help her with her lawyer. She's going to need a good one. I told her I'd talk to you about it first. It would mean a lot to me to do something to help her with that money."

"I think that's a good idea, babe. Got no problem with that. Her man sounds like a piece of shit. But I gotta ask, are you ever gonna wanna use it for yourself? For Mad?" he countered, his tone quiet but firm.

We hadn't touched a dime of my trust and though Axel didn't seem to care about the money, he cared about why I didn't want to touch it.

"We don't need it," I shrugged, hoping he'd let me off easy.

"That's not why you don't want to touch it," he countered, his hand grasping my hair for a moment before continuing his perusal through its strands.

"No," I murmured, agreeing with him.

"Why then?" He pressed his lips against my temple.

"Because of what it did to me my whole life." I shuddered.

"So let's say we use that money to pay for your school if you decide to go back, you gonna become your mother?" his tone was teasing, but I knew he was asking a serious question.

"No," I shook my head.

"You gonna change the way you love Mad? The way you love me?"

"No," I repeated, realizing his simple reasoning was actually getting through to me.

"It's just money, babe. The danger or value is what you do with it; what you let it do to you."

I looked up at him in the dim light taking in his words.

He gave me a small smile before continuing, "So I'm all right with you helping Jill. I owe the woman more than I can say for helping you when you had no one. But I want you to get to a place where you're not afraid of it – the money I mean. If that's the case, then it's controlling you just as much as it always did."

Holy hell, he was totally right. He knew me so well.

"You're right," I admitted, voicing my thoughts aloud. "I don't want that," I shook my head.

"It's the last of your trust," his deep voice rumbled.

"What do you mean?"

"The money," he shrugged, "you don't trust it. You think it will change us. I want to see you let that shit go. Believe in our family, in what we have," he growled.

"I do," I answered fervently.

"Prove it," he dared. "I don't give a fuck what you do with it. Spend it on Jill, spend it on stupid shit, just don't be afraid of it. Don't think that something as fucking trivial as money could change us," he demanded, his voice stronger now.

I had been afraid of that. I realized then that it couldn't change us. Change me. The very fact he could voice my fears aloud, fears I hadn't even fully articulated myself, therein lay the difference between what I'd known for most of my life and what we had. Axel understood me better than myself.

He wanted me to be free.

If it was possible, I loved him even more in that very moment.

"Nothing can change us," I whispered, my lips finding that sweet spot on his collarbone. "Love you, babe," I breathed, my lips moving higher to his gorgeous mouth.

He pulled me over his body, my legs straddling him as he gripped my upper thighs. "Prove it," he dared with one of his rare ear-to-ear grins.

Chapter Twenty-Two

Unsurprisingly, Axel didn't go for the whole Jill watching Maddox idea, which is how I found myself holding our very cranky baby in the midst of a very rowdy celebration the following evening.

The club was packed inside with only a few braving the chilly evening to smoke out back. The music blared and drinks were flowing. Axel had been at the club for most of the day, but later collected us from home. I'd tried to tell him once before that maybe Mad and I should stay home but he'd been adamant that we be a part of the celebration, even for just a little while.

I'd passed my driver's test and would have felt comfortable driving, but we hadn't gotten around to picking out a car and Axel seemed to feel better that I not drive alone just yet, which I understood.

Well, most days anyway. This party at the club was a perfect example of where I just wanted to pop in, say hello and take my baby home to bed.

There were scantily clad women everywhere fawning over Ryker and the few remaining single men. I sat with Connie watching my brother-in-law soak up the limelight.

"He's not having any fun," Connie noted drolly.

I laughed. "Clearly not one for the spotlight," I nodded with a grin, glad to see Ry so happy.

The grin fell away as I set eyes on my brother. His dark gaze searched the room landing on Axel as his legs ate the space to get closer. I watched him stride across the room his fists clenched and expression grim.

The two men exchanged words with both their eyes glancing my way more than once. I could see a clear "fuck" slip from Axel's lips.

Well, that couldn't be good.

Axel turned on his heel walking toward me with measured steps. His expression was difficult to read as his eyes met mine.

"What happened?" I demanded, my heart racing as I held Maddox closer. The noise and commotion around us was suddenly overwhelming. I felt like I couldn't breathe as panic set in.

My eyes shot between my husband and my brother, beseeching one of them to tell me what the hell was going on.

"Soph," Sal's voice was full of sympathy and concern as he regarded me.

That really scared me. My brother was many things. Sympathetic wasn't one of the emotions I'd seen in him before.

"Tell me what the hell is going on!" I demanded, my eyes wide.

"C'mere," Axel coaxed as quietly as the noise in the room would allow. He took my hand leading me back toward the offices. I held Maddox with my other arm focusing on the warmth and solidity of his little body.

Sal followed us, his hands shoved in his pockets his

head hung low.

"I want to take you home," Axel stated when we'd rid ourselves of the crowd.

"You want to drive all the way home without telling me what's happening?" I demanded incredulously.

He sighed, his hand cupping the back of his neck looking to the ceiling as though it would provide him with an answer.

Studying them both, my eyes shot between them. This wasn't about an impending threat. No, this was something different. They were upset – for me.

Suddenly I knew.

"It's my father, isn't it?" I choked out with stunning clarity. My limbs began to shake when they didn't rush to dispute me.

"Come here, buddy." Sal held his arms out for Mad, taking his weight from me and holding him close.

I looked to Axel, my eyes imploring him as he pulled me close, his chin resting on the top of my head.

"I'm sorry, baby," he whispered.

I squeezed my eyes shut, trying desperately to grapple with what his apology meant.

My father was dead.

The imposing, larger-than-life figure who had ruled so much of my life. He was…gone. He hadn't been warm. He'd been distant and stern. He expected so much and gave nothing in return. He always had his own agenda that much had been made especially clear in the last year. But, he was still my dad.

I was overwhelmed with the fact that he'd been wiped from the earth.

"He's…" I couldn't say the words as I clutched the

fabric of Axel's t-shirt in my fist.

"Yeah, baby he's gone. I'm sorry," he replied, his hand clutching my hair pulling me closer.

I looked up at him through tears, surprised by his sympathy. "You're sorry?" I queried.

"Sophie," his voice was hoarse as his grey eyes lit with emotion peering down at me. "Does this hurt you?"

I nodded.

"Then, baby, I am sorry," he emphasized the words, his expression pierced with sincerity.

"What happened?" I asked hoarsely.

Axel and Sal exchanged a look as though unsure what to share.

"He was killed, Soph," Sal's voice returned as Maddox squealed, pulling his lip.

My child's squeal of delight was such an odd contrast to the solemnity in the room.

"Killed how?" I pressed, pulling away from Axel and crossing my arms protectively around myself.

"Murdered," Sal admitted quietly.

I nodded numbly, tears spilling over.

"Let me take you home. I'll tell you what I know with you wrapped up in our bed," Axel coaxed quietly.

"I'll follow you," Ry was suddenly in the doorway, his expression grim. "I'll watch this guy," his chin lifted to Mad.

"Me too," Jill added, stepping in behind Ry.

Clearly, news had spread.

"But this is your night," I protested, wiping my face with the back of my hand.

"This night's about what it means to have a family," Ry returned. "You're family," he shrugged before his eyes turned to his brother. "Take her home, man. Take my bike. I'll put Mad in your truck and be right behind you."

Axel nodded. "Let's go, baby," he murmured, wrapping an arm around me and guiding me into the chilly night beyond.

As soon as we arrived home, Axel led me through the dark house to our room. He started a shower, letting the warm water steam up the space.

He undressed me without a word, his large hands finding every button, every clasp without any help from me.

He led us under the spray and held me close as the water rushed over us.

His large hands found their way into my hair as he washed it, his fingers rubbing through my scalp.

He said all he could without words. His body enshrouded mine, anchoring me while I fought against an emotional sea.

We stood under the spray until the water turned cold. Then he guided me out, drying me carefully. He led me into our dark bedroom, drawing the covers back and guiding me underneath.

I only lost him for a moment while he turned out the bathroom light and slid in to meet me.

Still we didn't speak.

I listened to the sounds of our home, of Ryker and Jill murmuring to each other quietly in the living room.

I tried to grasp the reality that my father was gone.

"He was so awful and I'm so sad," I admitted brokenly, finally after what must have been hours of silence.

"I know, baby," he replied, holding me closer still.

"What happened?" I managed to ask.

The silence stretched for many long moments. "We don't know everything yet. I can only guess that someone didn't want the police to find him first," he surmised grimly. "Or for our club to be able to ask him questions," he added. "There were a lot of loose ends we wanted him to tie up including who was feeding him inside information."

"Is my mother okay? Does she know?" I demanded.

"Sal's checking on her now," he assured me.

I groaned, confused and conflicted. "Why do I feel so worried? So sad? When they were nothing but awful to me and Sal?"

"I wish it were as simple as that, babe," he sighed. "I wish you could remember that, – have it take away your pain. That's not who you are." He sighed.

"He didn't want Maddox to exist, yet I can't believe he never laid eyes on his only grandchild," I murmured sorrowfully.

He simply pulled me tighter. Really, there were no words to soothe my chaotic emotions.

"Did the Black Riders do this?" I demanded after a few long moments.

"We don't know," he admitted. "Maybe," he added hesitantly.

"If they did?" I questioned.

He sighed and I heard his hand rustle over his beard. "If they did, then it depends on why, Soph. It could mean war," he admitted.

"That doesn't sound good," I squeaked out.

"No," he agreed. "Cal is on it, along with the rest of the guys."

"And you're here with me," I interjected, the realization finally dawning on me.

"Yeah," he replied.

I pulled away from his body, looking down into his face. "You don't want to be with them?" I asked.

He grunted. "There'll be a time," he assured me with a nod, pulling me back down to him. "But I realized something recently. My loyalty and my love for the club – it doesn't mean anything if I don't have your back," he explained quietly.

My heart thudded impatiently at his words, hungry to swallow them whole.

"I'll always have your back too," I assured him.

"I know. Can you sleep?" he murmured, his lips against my temple.

"Maybe," I sighed, feeling completely wrung out. "If you're here," I added.

"Nowhere else I would be, babe," he assured me, his bare skin warming mine.

"I love you," I sighed.

"Love you," he returned, kissing my hair.

I drifted off on a wave that crested between sleep and wakefulness. My father's image persisted in my mind as a shadow in the periphery of my childhood. It wasn't until I focused on the image of Axel holding Maddox that I drifted off in peace. Imagining my husband hold and love our child through my sleep muddled brain brought a smile across my lips.

Axel had given me that – peace.

That and so much more.

Chapter Twenty-Three

"I want that one. Our ceiling is high enough," I stated, hands on my hips as Axel eyed me warily. We'd been scouring the Christmas tree lot for the perfect tree for going on an hour and clearly he was over it.

It had been a week since my father died. Every day I worked to accept that he was actually gone. The hardest part was the lack of closure. On some level, I realized I'd hoped to have that with him. To at least understand what had driven him to do all the things he'd done. I'd have to find that closure within myself. It would take time.

Things with the Black Riders were still uncertain. Axel hadn't shared much but I knew if there was immediate danger, he'd tell me. For the time being, the guys were pretty guarded on the details. Frankly, I didn't have the capacity to deal with it anyway and didn't ask. I trusted Axel to take care of it.

The holidays were a welcomed distraction. I'd decorated the house with close to an obnoxious amount of cheer. Ax had helped where he could and stayed out of the way when he needed to, which was often. I was determined to have our first Christmas as a family be as close to perfect as possible.

"Baby, that thing is like ten feet tall," Axel groused, craning his neck to look at the tree I had in mind.

"So?" I queried with my head cocked to the side.

"You gonna lug it through the lot into the truck and then into the house?" he demanded.

"Well, no," I replied, biting my lip and eyeing the tree again to see if maybe I could somehow do just that.

He chuckled, shaking his head at my antics. Maddox whined in the backpack I had him strapped in. He was over it too.

"Fine, we can find a slightly smaller one," I gave in, giving him my best dejected expression.

"Christ," he muttered, shaking his head. "Fine."

"Yay!" I clapped my hands together.

"You and those damn big eyes," he lamented. "If we have a girl, I'm seriously screwed."

"Yeah you are," I agreed, suddenly wanting to give him just that.

******

"That's a big fucking tree," Sal commented when he and Kat came over later that evening.

"It's gorgeous," Kat smiled, elbowing Sal in the ribs. She scooped Mad up off the floor trying to position him over her burgeoning belly.

"Jesus, babe, don't try to hold him. He's too heavy," Sal argued, seeming stressed as he pried my son from her arms.

She rolled her eyes but let him take Maddox. I was surprised my brother hadn't had a heart attack at some point during her pregnancy. He was constantly prying things out of her arms or making her sit down. It was sweet, but I knew Kat was at the end of her rope.

I winked at her from the kitchen where I was attempting to cook an edible dinner. I was determined not to poison everyone.

When Ry and Jill let themselves in, they were in the middle of an argument, not an uncommon occurrence for them. They'd become good friends and often bickered like siblings.

"Do you know how hard it is to find good childcare?" Jill was saying as they swept into the room. "Hi," she paused to greet Kat and me with a hug before continuing her rant. "Seriously, Ry," she huffed. "Piper works at the best daycare in town. There are so many willing chicks in this town. Can't you go try to screw one of them? You can't pull your typical shit with Piper. She's not like that and then I'll have to find somewhere else for Mason." Jill added, looking stressed.

If I didn't know any better, I'd think he looked hurt by the accusation. "Maybe I don't want to just fuck her," he muttered.

Well, that was just plain shocking. The weighted silence in the room confirmed as much.

"Are you sick? Do you need a doctor?" Sal goaded him.

"What's this now?" Axel asked, coming into the room.

"Ry seems to have a boner for Jill's babysitter, Piper," Sal muttered, stifling a laugh.

Axel's brows rose in surprise. "Piper Owens?"

"You know her?" Jill asked, confused.

"Sure, Ry went to school with her. He was pulling her pigtails in second grade," Axel chuckled. "She and Ry were thick as thieves 'til she moved away after high school.

I didn't realize she was back in town," he added, coming to put an arm around me and dropping a quick kiss to my temple. "Haven't seen her since the funeral," he added somberly. "That was what, a year ago now?"

Ry looked up at the ceiling with a clenched jaw. "Yeah, I didn't realize she was back either until I dropped the Mace man off for Jill."

"She won't give you the time of day?" Axel guessed with a quirked brow.

"Ah, the way many epic romances begin," Kat grinned.

Ryker's eyes shot downward, looking uncomfortable, a rarity for Ryker.

"Shit, is that a blush? Is he blushing?" Jill demanded. "I'm so screwed," she groaned.

I'd say that was a very fair assessment.

"Let's have dinner," I cut in, wanting to save Ryker from his apparent misery.

He shot me a grateful look and nodded enthusiastically at my suggestion.

We sat down for dinner with no more talk of Piper and no one outwardly grimaced as they began to eat which I took as a good sign.

When the doorbell rang, I was surprised since we didn't expect anyone else. I rose to answer it but Axel stopped me with a look.

"I'll get it," he said gruffly, scooting his chair back with a screech as he moved to the door.

I couldn't stop my intake of breath when I saw who was on the other side of the door.

My mother stood underneath the porch light, clutching her jacket around her uncertainly.

"Please don't turn me away," she rushed to say.

Axel just stared at her in shock, unsure how to respond.

"What are you doing here?" Sal growled as he glared at our mother.

"Everyone just relax," I commanded, holding up my hand for them to be quiet as I stood to move to Axel's side. "Come in," I beckoned after a moment more of deliberation. I was curious what she wanted, and despite how she'd treated me, I wasn't prepared to turn her away cold on our doorstep.

She gave me a small nod and stepped into our great room, her eyes darting warily around the space.

"I can come back another time. It looks like you're having dinner," she nodded to the dining room table.

"We are," I replied, noticing how her eyes clung to Maddox as she took him in. "But come in," I added after a pause.

"What do you want?" Sal cut in again, having far less patience for her and her presence here.

Suddenly, her eyes shot wide before she composed herself. "You're...expecting?" She swallowed, looking at Kat.

Kat nodded as Sal put a protective arm around her.

My mother clenched her hands more tightly around her coat, seeming at a loss for what to say. "You didn't come to the funeral," she commented finally, her eyes shifting to me and then to Sal.

"No," I shook my head simply, as though daring her to challenge us.

"I understand," she nodded, surprising me. "He'd alienated nearly everyone we knew toward the end. But he was my husband," she shrugged dejectedly, showing a rare moment of vulnerability. "He was my husband," she repeated quietly as though to herself. She took a moment, straightening her shoulders and clearing her throat.

"I told you the last time I saw you that I've had time to reflect since you've been gone," she murmured, looking to me. Then her eyes swept to Sal. "And for you," she swallowed. "I lost you so long ago." She shook her head. "I'm sorry it's taken me so long to realize how important it is to make that right. You two and the families you're building, well, you're all I have left," she spoke quickly, as though rushing to get the words past her lips.

"Is this because you're broke?" Sal cut in harshly.

"Sal," Kat murmured in an effort to calm him. I was relieved she stepped in. Though I understood his hostility, it wasn't helping at the moment.

"After everything your father did, that's fair," she allowed. "But no, I'm not broke. I started saving my own money years ago when I first suspected Richard was doing some questionable things," she shared, referring to my father. "I had no idea you weren't getting your money," she shook her head.

"We know," I assured her.

She sighed, her body deflating in relief that I seemed to believe her.

"I went to see your father," she shared, turning to look at Sal.

Well, that was certainly a surprise. Sal's father lived in Spain. I didn't know the whole story other than she'd had some type of affair with him when she was young and fell pregnant with Sal.

"Why the fuck did you do that?" he demanded.

"Sal," I murmured in a quiet plea for him to lighten up.

"That's between him and me," she answered defensively, her crisp demeanor returning in a bid to protect herself, no doubt.

In a weird way, I was relieved to see that cool attitude return. It was what I was familiar with at least.

"What I want you to know is that I'm trying." She cleared her throat demurely, looking uncomfortable with so many eyes on her. "I'm trying to repair the damage I know I've done. It started with Gael and the way I treated him. It was important to me that he knew I've always regretted it."

I'd never heard my mother admit regret or admit wrongdoing. The fact that she'd flown all the way to Spain to apologize to Sal's father really said something. It was then I felt a glimmer of hope that maybe she'd really changed.

"I want a chance to be in your lives," she stated firmly. "I'm your mother. I'm the only surviving family you two have. You're certainly all I have." She clasped her hands together, standing stiffly as she looked to me and then to Sal. "Please," she finished, her tone strong despite the fear in her eyes.

You could have heard a pin drop as the tension coiled thick. Even Maddox who constantly babbled and squealed was silent, seeming to sense the strain in the room.

Hurt flickered over her face as the silence stretched. "Okay," she nodded, seeming to accept our silence as rejection. "I'll go," she swallowed, turning to leave.

I looked to Sal, my eyes pleading. A silent understanding passed between us. If we were doing this, it would be together and it had to come from him.

"Fuck," he muttered, hanging his head for a moment.

"Wait," he instructed her gruffly.

She turned on her heel looking at him wearily.

"I don't know if it'll work after all the shit you put us both through," he began, looking to me briefly before his eyes shot back to our mother. "But I know something about needing redemption." He pulled Kat close and I knew he was thinking about having to fight his way back to her. "So I'm willing to give it a shot," he added brusquely.

Axel put his arm around my waist pulling me closer, telling me without words that he'd accept any decision I made.

"Me too," I spoke up when the eyes in the room had turned to me. Axel squeezed my hip in support.

"Thank you," she murmured.

"How long are you in town for?" I asked.

She gave a small shrug. "Indefinitely. Things are a bit up in the air right now."

"Why don't you come by tomorrow?" I offered. I wasn't ready to invite her for dinner. We'd need to do this a little bit at a time. "We could have coffee or something."

Her eyes lit with a spark of hope. "I'd like that," she replied. "I'll let you get on with your evening," she added, heading toward the door. I followed her toward the door opening it to the chilly evening air. I watched her thin form move to her rental car and sent a silent plea that she wouldn't make us regret giving her a chance. It was huge for Sal to give her this opportunity – I didn't want to see him hurt.

She gave a small wave before driving off down the road.

That evening, Axel and I cleaned up together. Dinner had been a success, well no one had died anyway and the meal had been somewhat edible. After my mom left, we hadn't talked about the visit; instead, we kept the mood light.

"It was good, babe," Axel's deep voice assured me as he moved in behind me to kiss my neck. He smelled like beer and pumpkin pie, a surprisingly delicious combination. "You taste good. I've been waiting all night to get my mouth on you," he growled against my skin.

I froze mid-rinse from my place at the sink and leaned into his mouth.

His arms wrapped around my middle pulling me back against his firm body.

In one quick movement, my leggings were pulled down and off. He moved us quickly to the opposite counter, his large body imposing and deliciously hard behind mine.

"Spread," he ordered, his mouth against my shoulder.

I shuddered with anticipation as I followed his demand. His hand immediately moved to my core, his fingers sliding through the moisture that he'd immediately created as his other hand moved to my covered breast.

His fingers moved expertly, bringing me to the brink of orgasm within seconds. I leaned my head back against his shoulder and moaned.

"That's right, baby. I want to hear you," he rasped in my ear as he quickened his movements.

His other hand found my nipple through my clothes, squeezing with just the right amount of pressure. The man could play my body like an instrument.

I erupted with a cry that echoed off the walls, shuddering in his arms.

He held me for a second before pushing me back to the counter guiding me to lay my top half down. I spread my arms out in front of me and pressed my cheek against the cool counter top.

The anticipation was heady as he moved in behind me. Hearing the sound of his zipper was just about the sexiest sound I'd ever heard.

"Oh, God," I croaked, more than ready for him.

He moved my legs farther apart seconds before he entered me in one fluid thrust.

He felt impossibly big and deliciously deep as he found a rhythm set to make me lose my mind.

I loved the feeling of his jeans against my bare thighs, of his hands at my waist in a grip so tight it was sure to cause a few bruises.

They'd be worth it.

His hands moved to my shoulders pulling me back into him as he thrust deeper and faster. "Fuck," he bit out, his breathing labored and harsh as he took me hard.

I groaned low and loud, close to another climax.

"That's right," he responded, knowing I was close. "God, you're so fucking hot, baby," he rasped.

His words were enough to send me over, pulling him with me.

He collapsed on top of me, pressing me harder into the counter as we caught our breath.

He kissed the side of my neck before he lifted off me, leaning down to pull my leggings back up my legs. "You should wear these more often," he commented as I turned to watch him tuck himself back in his jeans.

I smothered a smile. "Oh?" I asked quirking a brow.

He nodded. "I get to stare at that sweet ass all night and then…easy access," he grinned, pulling me in for a kiss.

"Right," I laughed, throwing my arms around him. He

lifted me so my legs followed suit.

"Let's hit the shower," he said, walking us toward the bedroom. "I'm not done," he added, biting my earlobe before licking away the sting.

"No?" I asked breathlessly.

"Far from it," he growled into my neck, making my tired limbs come alive once more.

He spoke and my body answered; it was that simple.

It was hours later and we were lying tangled in each other's arms, satiated and exhausted. My eyelids were heavy as I moved closer to sleep. "You think I did the right thing?" I asked quietly, my hand moving over the plane of his chest.

Without explanation, he knew what I meant.

I felt him shrug. "No way to know, babe. She'll have to prove it. If you weren't so strong and you didn't have the kind of support you do, I'd worry more about it."

"But I have you," I smiled up at him.

"You have me," he affirmed gruffly, pulling me up for a kiss. "Always."

Chapter Twenty-Four

It was three days before Christmas when I was awoken unexpectedly from a deep sleep. "Babe, your phone," Axel's voice cut through the darkness.

"Hmm?" I mumbled. Lately, I'd been sleeping like the dead.

"Your phone, it's ringing," he repeated, moving into the room. He was still up so I couldn't have been asleep for very long.

My hand reached blindly for the nightstand, noting blearily that it was only 11 p.m. I had just fallen asleep but it felt like hours ago. "Hello?" I rasped.

"Kat's in labor. We're headed into the hospital. Can you meet me there?" Sal's voice came urgently through the line.

I sat up abruptly, suddenly wide-awake. "Yes! I'll be there as soon as I can," I answered, thrilled that my niece was on her way.

I disconnected and clicked on the light, moving at hyper speed to find my clothes.

"Can you stay with Mad?" I asked urgently.

"Yeah," he nodded. "I want you to be really careful driving down the mountain. The roads are slick," he warned.

"I will," I nodded. I'd been driving regularly in what I affectionately called "The Tank." Axel had claimed my ginormous SUV was safer on the mountain and had plenty of "space." That man and the brood he wanted.

I rolled my eyes at the time, but I had to admit I did feel safer in it.

He kissed me tenderly, his fingers running through my hair. "Relax for me a bit. I don't want you driving like this," he said against my lips. His methods for relaxation usually worked like a charm and this was no different.

"Okay," I sighed, wishing I could delay for a bit longer.

He grinned knowingly, delivering a swift smack to my ass.

"Hey!" I protested with a grin.

"Later," he nodded, his eyes full of promise.

My knees went weak. "Later," I agreed breathlessly.

Thirty minutes later, I was pulling up to the hospital and running through the halls like a madwoman.

When I spotted Jill looking adorable in her hospital scrubs, I immediately sighed with relief. We hadn't known if she'd be on shift when Kat went into labor. She'd been working at the hospital for a few weeks and seemed to love it. Her divorce was ugly but we'd gotten her a kickass lawyer. The outlook was good for her to get full custody of Mason.

"You're here," I breathed, hugging her.

"My only swing shift this week," she nodded with a smile. "Piper's with Mason so I can stay until the baby comes."

"That's great. Kat will be so glad," I smiled. "Ry still seem interested in her?" I asked as we headed down the long brightly lit hallway.

She looked thoughtful. "It's more than that. We all may have misjudged him on this one," she admitted. "I think he really cares about her. I feel badly for giving him so much shit," she smiled ruefully.

Well, that was something. I wanted to meet this Piper.

"How's Kat?" I asked as a baby's wail ricocheted off the walls.

"Great. She's progressing relatively fast with it being her first baby," she explained as we arrived at their room.

Kat was sitting up in bed with Sal leaning over her. His forehead was pressed to hers and I waited quietly, not wanting to interrupt the moment between them.

"Hey, you're here," Kat smiled when she saw me.

"I'm here," I nodded with a grin. "Okay?" I asked, my eyes shooting to Sal.

"I'm just telling this guy to chill," Kat replied, quirking her thumb at my brother.

"I am chill," he argued.

"Right," I nodded, trying to keep the sarcasm from my tone as Jill moved around the room checking vitals and noting a few things in Kat's chart.

As it turned out, my brother was the epitome of calm. He was an unyielding source of support for his wife throughout her relatively short but intense labor.

It wasn't until my niece came screaming into the world, the top of her head a mass of dark hair that I saw him take a shaky breath, his mask of calm slipping.

"She's gorgeous," his voice rasped with emotion as he looked down at his daughter in awe.

"What's her name?" I asked as I peeked over his shoulder at my niece. I was biding my time until I got to hold her.

"Wren," he answered, winking at Kat.

"That's so perfect," I clapped my hands together. Sal had affectionately called Kat "birdie" for as long as I'd known them as a couple. No one could say how it started. It was just one of those things. It was perfectly fitting that they'd name their daughter after a bird.

It wasn't long before it felt like the entire club was filling the room, everyone waiting their turn to meet the new arrival.

When Axel walked in, I beamed at him wanting to share this incredible moment with him.

"She's so beautiful," I announced proudly after he'd pulled me into his arms and kissed me soundly.

"Oh, yeah?" he grinned.

"Yeah," I nodded. "Mad?"

"He's with Ry," he replied, his gaze turning to the littlest member of our extended family. "Look at that hair," he chuckled.

"There's a lot of it," I agreed with a grin as Sal finally placed her in my arms. I'd been waiting, rather impatiently, since she'd been born.

"She looks so much like you, man," Axel said, looking down at the tiny bundle nestled in my arms.

"You think?" Sal grinned, practically bursting with pride.

"She'll be gorgeous just like her mama," I winked over at Kat who was smiling tiredly at us all. "I think we should let these two ladies get some beauty sleep," I added, noticing exactly how exhausted Kat looked. It was a lot of commotion after having just given birth.

"Good idea," Sal nodded. "You'll stay?" he asked Jill

as she swept by checking on Kat.

Jill had been amazing throughout the whole birth and I didn't blame Sal for not wanting her far. I wouldn't be surprised if he tried to convince her to move in.

"I'll stay awhile longer," she assured him, grasping his hand briefly with a warm smile.

She was completely in her element. I was so proud of her.

"We'll be by tomorrow if you're not discharged by then. Otherwise, we'll bring some food by the house," I told Sal, giving him a quick hug. He wasn't typically much of a hugger but I couldn't help myself. "I'll buy some prepared food," I added with an eye roll when I saw the look of apprehension on his face.

"Thanks, sis," he replied, hugging me back briefly before turning his attention to his family.

I looked at Sal and marveled at how much he'd changed from the brother I'd caught glimpses of as a kid. He was still gruff and at times distant, I had no doubt that would always be the case to some degree, but he was also centered in a way I hadn't seen before. He was happy from the inside out; he just showed it in his own way. Love had done that for him. It had done the same for me.

"Want to go home?" I murmured to Axel as he wrapped an arm around me.

"Yeah, baby," he nodded. "Let's take the bike. Someone can bring your car back later," he added.

"Sounds perfect," I replied with an exalted grin. I freaking loved that bike and the man who rode it.

"I think we should start the expansion project on the house," I mused as we walked down the hospital halls toward the exit.

"Oh, yeah?" he cocked a brow.

I shrugged innocently, knowing my suggestion resonated with him. It meant my letting go of the past and moving toward our future.

He stopped me as we reached the parking lot, stooping to look into my eyes. "You lettin' it go?" he asked.

I swallowed against the ball of emotion suddenly choking me. I wouldn't ever fully get over the loss of my father and we still didn't know who'd killed him. I still had a long road with my mother. But with Axel by my side, propping me up, I felt like I could do anything. The truth was that with the love of a great man I *could* do anything.

"Yeah, babe," I grinned. "Now are you gonna take me for a ride?"

He licked his lips, his eyes perusing my form in a way that made my heart pound and knees go weak.

"We'll take the long way," he growled into my neck.

In so many ways, we had taken the long way around, but in that time, we'd come together far stronger than I'd ever thought possible. It was time to hold tightly to my man for whatever the future held and always remember to enjoy the ride along the way.

Epilogue

One Month Later

"**M**om?" I called as I walked through our house. It was a bit of a disaster with the construction we'd started and I was ready to have my home back – well a bigger version of it anyway.

"In here," her voice called from the nursery.

I found my son and mother sitting on the floor looking at books. Maddox squealed when he saw me, crawling over to be picked up. I scooped him up kissing his sweet neck and smiled.

"How did you two do?" I asked, tickling his belly.

"Great," she smiled, rising to her feet.

Ever since that visit over six weeks ago, we'd been letting her spend time at the house. It was only recently we began leaving her alone with Maddox for any length of time. Maddox adored her and the feeling was mutual.

"Do you want to stay for dinner?" I offered as she followed me into the kitchen.

"I would but Sal wanted me to help with Wren for an

hour or so tonight," she shared with a bright smile.

I knew that was huge for her. My brother had been decidedly more cautious about letting our mother near his family. Slowly but surely, he was coming around as she proved on a daily basis that people could change. He knew it was possible since he himself had already proven that ten times over.

"That's great. Give her a kiss for me. I'll be over there tomorrow," I replied as I tried to keep my slightly frazzled state under wraps.

"Everything okay?" she asked.

Hopefully.

"Yep," I nodded far too quickly.

She didn't press. Our relationship had dramatically improved to something far healthier than we'd ever had, but we still had a way to go.

I walked her out hearing my phone buzz from the other room.

Is he home yet?

Have you told him?

Jill's persistent texts made me sigh with exasperation. It had been all of twenty minutes since I'd seen her.

I was also irritated with her constantly dodging my questions about her love life. Her divorce was in full swing, but she'd settled in comfortably in Hawthorne. She loved her job and had daycare for Mason. I wanted to see her have some fun.

Not yet

I typed quickly, setting my phone aside and beginning to make dinner while Maddox entertained himself with the Tupperware drawer. He was growing up so fast; he'd be walking any day. I couldn't believe it.

Axel strode in as I was putting the casserole in the oven. He'd been spending more hours at the club as the guys worked to solve what the cops weren't. There were no official answers about my father's murder, but every day, it looked more and more like it had been the Black Riders. The consequences of that were daunting at best.

"Hi, baby," his deep voice rumbled and he kissed my neck.

"Hi," I replied, trying to hide my nervous energy.

"Hey, little man," he greeted Maddox, scooping him up.

Maddox squealed in delight as Axel carried him off to survey the work completed on the house during the day. It was part of his routine; he did a walk through with Mad sometimes in the middle of the day if he could find the time. We were adding an entire second story. It would take months but the result would double our square footage.

"What'd you do today?" he asked when he'd returned, grabbing a beer from the fridge.

I dropped the knife I'd been holding, startled by his question.

"Jesus, babe, be careful," he cursed, bending to pick it up. "You all right?" he asked concerned.

"Fine, why wouldn't I be fine?" I replied hurriedly.

He looked at me skeptically. "Are you on the rag?" he demanded.

I let out a choking sound, something between a laugh and a cough. "Uh no, why?"

"'Cause you get a little crazy when you're on the rag," he shrugged, eyeing me steadily.

"Nope," I shook my head. "Just must be in a weird mood," I added breezily. "My mom and Mad had fun," I added, changing the subject.

"Oh?"

I nodded. "I ran out for just about an hour. Oh, and Sal wanted her to come help with Wren." I grinned.

He smiled. "That's great, baby."

"Yeah," I sighed. "Dinner will be ready soon," I added, shooing him out of the kitchen. Until Mad went to bed, avoidance was my method of choice and I was rolling with that as long as my far too perceptive man would let me get away with it.

"Okay, baby, what gives?" he demanded in exasperation later that night. I'd spent the evening a bumbling distracted mess. We'd put Maddox to bed and I knew I couldn't avoid it any longer.

I bit my lip. "I have something to tell you and I'm nervous," I blurted.

"Okay," he nodded warily, waiting for me to continue.

"I got you a present," I said, rising from the bed to grab it.

"A present?" his brow wrinkled in confusion.

"Open it," I said softly, handing him the gift bag and standing nervously, fighting the urge to pace.

He removed the tissue paper and pulled out the tiny onesie I'd picked up earlier that day. In black letters, it read, "I have the world's best Daddy."

He looked at it in consternation for a minute. "But this is too small for..." Then I saw the light go on and he looked up at me in wonder. "Does this mean what I think it means?"

I bit my lip and nodded.

He swallowed hard as his eyes swept my frame landing on my belly. "You're givin' me another baby?" he demanded.

I nodded again.

From his place perched on the edge of the bed, he reached out and pulled me between his legs, his head resting on my flat belly.

"Eyes baby. I need your eyes," he demanded softly.

I looked down stunned at the emotion that looked back at me. "I just wasn't sure," I murmured. "If you'd be ready. It's so much sooner than we'd talked about."

"Well, we haven't been exactly great about birth control," he chuckled.

That was an understatement. There were many times we'd been careless. Part of me thought on some level we'd both wanted this to happen.

I blushed, remembering how fun all those times had been.

He looked up at me with pure joy lighting his face. "I'm fucking thrilled," he rasped, laying a kiss to my belly.

I sighed, feeling all of my earlier nerves and apprehension leave me in a rush. "Me too," I grinned. "Jill ran a test for me at the hospital, but I waited for any type of exam until you could come," I explained.

"Good," he nodded approvingly, his fingers tracing up under my t-shirt exploring the skin underneath. "Another baby," he murmured with a grin. "I can't wait to see you get round. I can't wait to be there for it all. This time, I'm not missing anything," he said emphatically.

"I know," I assured him, stroking my fingers through his thick hair.

"Thank you, baby, you've given me everything," his voice grated with emotion. "Everything."

"I'm glad you feel that way, honey," I swallowed,

bending to touch his lips with mine. "Because we're just getting started."

The End

Thank you for reading!

The Ride Series continues with the story of Piper and Ryker. Available now!

To find more information on the Ride Series, Megan O'Brien's other titles, and ways to follow and connect with Megan, please visit:

meganobrienbooks.com

Megan O'Brien is the best selling author of the Ride Series and the Talon Security Series. She has a passion for a good love story and most enjoys writing stories with an alpha male and strong female characters.

Megan was born and raised in Marin County, California where she still resides with her amazing husband and three lovely children.

When she's not enjoying family time or burying her nose in her kindle she loves hiking, running and relaxing moments on the back porch with a glass of wine.

Fall in love with all the men of the Knights MC in the Ride Series!

Follow the men of Talon Security as the ex military security specialists work together to protect the women they love and each other in this contemporary romance series.

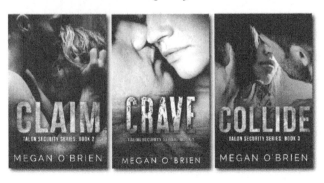

Made in the USA
Monee, IL
13 September 2023

42688262R00144